A DEADLY SHADE OF ROSE

DOUGLAS HIRT

WOLFPACK
PUBLISHING
— EST 2013 —

WOLFPACK
PUBLISHING
— EST 2013 —

A Deadly Shade of Rose

Paperback Edition
Copyright © 2020 Douglas Hirt

Wolfpack Publishing
6032 Wheat Penny Avenue
Las Vegas, NV 89122

Paperback ISBN: 978-1-64734-524-2
Ebook ISBN: 978-1-64734-039-1

A DEADLY SHADE OF ROSE

CHAPTER 1

Somewhere in the Colorado Rocky Mountains
March, 1983

No one would ever accuse the Italians of building fine military rifles. They do manage to turn out some excellent shotguns, and a few really nice handguns too, particularly of the Old Western Style. But their rifles are probably some of the worst in the world, especially those sloppy smoke poles turned out during the war—the big one a couple wars back. The particular example I was looking at now was a major abomination; partly factory fault and partly amateur gunsmith fault...well, butcher gunsmith... well, maybe just butcher.

It happened to be a Carcano with a cracked stock. Someone had sawn the front third of the stock off in a failed attempt at *sporterizing* the piece. Cradled in what remained of the gouged piece of timber was a badly pitted barrel and receiver, originally blued or parkerized, I suppose. Now it showed a lot of white metal as most of the finish had worn away long ago. It had obviously taken a lot of abuse since its service days and had come away worse for the wear, not that it had been much of a rifle to begin with; certainly not of the quality of a vintage Mauser 98 or a Springfield 03. But then, as I said, the Italians were never known for classy military hardware. All together I wouldn't give ten bucks for a wheelbarrow load of Carcanos, and I've seen quite a few in my lifetime.

Generally, I don't get very emotional over fire-arms, but this particular example had tromped on the gas pedal of my heart, had brought a catch to my breathing. The rifle was, I decided, the worst of a bad bunch, and the reason for my sudden illogic was simple. Its worn and badly pitted barrel was pointed at a spot about midway down my sternum.

And then the coffee spilled out over the rim of my blue enameled cup onto the hot iron grate, sizzling and splashing all over my carefully banked bed of coals. I yelped and dropped the cup. My eye flicked away from the rifle for half a second. When I looked back the battered barrel had shifted, but the finger on the trigger had remained steady.

It was a slim finger attached to a pink hand be-longing to the arm of a young lady who might have been attractive had her tangled hair been washed and brushed and the mud scrubbed from her red cheeks. Different clothing would have helped with the overall appearance too. The tan parka was cut to accommodate a body much larger than her own. The tattered hem of a blue dress showing beneath it seemed definitely out of place in this cold, high mountain air. Although the attire looked out of place, the rifle in her hands appeared right at home.

And for that I was grateful because her wary eyes told a very different story. Having a gun pointed at your chest is frightening all on its own. Having that same gun in timid hands with a nervous trigger finger is terrifying.

They were blue eyes, by the way, narrowed to a hard crease that didn't quite mask the fear in them. Her blushing, cold-pink cheeks contrasted strangely with her eyes. The stringy hair was some shade of dark brown. Beyond that I couldn't decipher anything else.

Of course, all of this came about a lot faster than it sounds. From hearing the crackle of dried leaves under foot until this instant might have been all of five seconds. She'd walked out of the fir tree forest like she'd know me for years. She'd caught my startled look and then in a glance took in my camp site, her stare lingered a long, pitiful moment upon my crumpled sleeping bag, still warm, before coming back to me. The unhappy corners of her mouth drooped lower and her square jaw set with a determined shift.

"I've been watching from the trees. You're alone?" Her words were accompanied by puffs of steam in the cold morning air. Their tone demanded a reply from me.

"I was until a moment ago," I said carefully, an eye on her trigger finger, giving what I hoped would be a reassuring smile.

"Don't smart off with me, mister. You alone?" Her cold, pink fingers tightened around the sad little rifle. My breathing went still. In spite of its looks, I wasn't naive enough to underestimate the piece. The Carcano fired a 6.5 mm round that killed a lot of good men forty years ago, not to mention a good man in the White House about twenty-five or so years ago.

Carefully, slowly, I raised my free hand while setting the coffee pot back onto the iron grate. "Sorry ma'am. Didn't mean to upset you." I spoke slowly, respectfully, aware of the stirring of a memory that I'd long ago put to rest hoping it would stay there. But that's the problem with memories....

It had been another dawn, another time, in a place far away from this cold, clean Colorado mountainside. The place had been steaming and dripping, and I had been alone there too since my companion had suddenly become quite dead. The small group of men in military clothing who had put a permanent halt to his startled lunge for the M-16 rifle near his bedroll had basically asked me the same question she'd just asked, except their English hadn't been nearly as good. Their weapons, however, had been quite superior if not even uglier, and they had been of Chinese origin—well, Russian, actually—not Italian.

I shook off the past and focused on the brown-hair-blue-eyed woman with the rifle. I told her that this squatting position she'd caught me in was getting uncomfortable and could I please change it? She nodded and the rifle made a small movement, which I took to mean okay and eased back off my haunches onto the cold ground. The parka that swallowed her appeared warm enough, in a bulky sort of way, but the open-toed sandals and ruined nylon hose had to be pure misery. The nearly bare bluish legs that poked down from beneath the coat quivered. She was swaying a little and I saw her making an effort to catch her balance.

"Have you a weapon here?" She glanced at the tackle box and fishing pole I'd leaned against a tree the night before after hiking up from the stream below with two small trout. They'd gone right into the frying pan soon as I'd stirred up the fire enough for it to do its job.

I nodded toward the old pickup truck that had hauled me and the gear up from the highway yesterday afternoon. "Under the front seat. It's only a .22 but you're welcome to it if it'll put your mind at ease. In fact, take the truck if that's what you want. The tank is full and there's some cash in the ashtray."

Her view shifted back and her hard, contemplative eyes scrutinized me without revealing the thoughts behind them. After a moment the threatening gaze softened a bit. Her face didn't actually turn friendly, but she did seem less inclined to see how large a hole a 6.5 mm round would blow through the chest of a medium to large size human critter. "That's generous of you."

I shrugged. "That old truck is a small price to pay if I get to walk out of these mountains with my skin intact."

She said, "I just might do that. What are you doing up here anyway? And don't tell me you're fishing. Who goes fishing in the cold?"

"Heck ma'am, in some parts of the country ice fishing is a bigger sport than football. Generally you'll find it practiced more up north than down here in Colorado where the lakes don't really freeze over, at least not solid enough to where you can drive a truck out onto them and haul out a shack with a stove and a hole in the floor. Most fishing done hereabouts is of the active variety. Cast and reel, cast and reel. Keeps you warm on a cold March afternoon."

She laughed but there was no humor in it. "That's all I need now. A lecture on fishing from you."

I said, "No ma'am, that's not what you need. What you need right now is a cup of hot coffee, some food, and a safe place that's warm."

Bingo. I'd found the spot where she hurt the most. She licked her dry, chapped lips, the hard gaze softening further. "Well actually it was the smell of coffee that led me here...to you." The hostility was gone from her voice.

"Great. Remind me to never to brew up a pot of coffee on a cold morning. Who knows what I might lure out of these mountains next time?" I turned to the grocery box next to a camp chair. She went taut. I said, "Coffee cup." She was on alert again. She nodded and I reached into the bag and came out with a cup identical to the one that still lay in the dirt near my leg. I filled it and handed it to her.

She started to reach for the cup, then stopped. A sudden riveting stare revealed a return of whatever terror had come upon her of recent. Maybe I intended to grab her wrist? Maybe there was a pistol hidden under my coat, or a garrote up my sleeve, or whatever it was she thought me capable of?

"Just set it down there."

I did and she motioned me back from the fire. I couldn't see any point arguing about it with the muzzle of her rifle pointing at me. I had no intention of grabbing for her wrist, or any other part of her, but at the moment I doubted I was going to convince her of that.

She said, "More. Over there," and swung the barrel toward a nearby tree.

"Sure thing lady. You know you really don't need to be threatening the local wildlife with that thing. I'm just a friendly fisherman intending to do no harm to anyone except to the local trout population."

"I'll decide if and when I don't need this." Her menacing tone that told me she knew what she was doing. She was no sucker and would use the rifle if she felt it necessary. "Scoot your bottom over to that tree and keep your hands where I can see them."

"Yes ma'am. Just make yourself to home, why don't you? I'd offer you cream and sugar, but I left those back at the cabin." I moved to the indicated tree and sat beside my tackle box, my hands dutifully exposed and crossed over my knees in plain sight. She shuffled the rifle to her left hand, carefully picked up the hot tin cup and sipped cautiously all the while watching me over its blue rim.

She said, "You have any food around here?"

"Haven't gotten around to preparing breakfast yet, me-lady. Sorry for the inconvenience."

"Cut the glib prattle." She seemed to want to say more but cut it short at that. Frowning, she took another pull at the coffee cup. "What's your name?"

It was a move in the right direction. "Granger, ma'am. Paul Granger." And the natural progression when a conversation took this direction was for me to ask her the same.

She thought a moment as if weighing the ramifications. She must have decided it could do no harm, or maybe she was just taking the time to make something up? "Marcie Rose, if it makes any difference."

"It doesn't, and I'm not sure I'm glad to make your acquaintance."

She laughed.

Another move in the right direction. I said, "There's eggs, bacon, and some cheese in the cooler. Some Hatch's green chili too. I'm pretty basic when I head to the woods. If you want, I'll scramble them up. You can have another cup of coffee while you watch."

"All right but go easy on the chili." Her voice tone took a warning note. "And don't-"

"I know, I know. Don't do anything daring or stupid." I grinned. "Don't worry Miss—or is it Mrs.-?—Rose. I've got plans for the next thirty to forty years, thank you very much."

Her face remained stern and she stepped warily out of the way, moving like a mountain lion tasting the scent of man on the wind. Marcie Rose appeared a most competent woman, at least she was comfortable around firearms. I couldn't quite believe a lone, unarmed fisherman would be much of a threat to her, especially since she was the one packing heat and giving orders. Yet it was plain she was one scared woman. Afraid of what? What had frightened her enough to have driven here out into the mountains on a cold March morning dressed as if she'd just come home from the office—except for the baggy parka that obviously did not belong to her. I suspected the rifle didn't either.

I invaded the Coleman cooler and removed breakfast fixings. I didn't have to look at her to know she was shifting foot to foot trying to keep warm. "The keys are in the ignition," I said keeping busy with the important work of getting a hot breakfast ready. "It's not much of a truck if you judge trucks by the plushy, soft sprung comfort buggies rolling off the assembly lines in Detroit or Hiroshima, or wherever it is they build them nowadays, but it takes me where I want to go, and it has a heck of a heater. Crawl inside, fire her up, and stick your toes down by it while I cook us something to eat."

She didn't say anything and she didn't move. Putting out of mind a rifle pointed at your back is no easy accomplishment. Not knowing her—not knowing her frame of mind—made the arrangement precarious, but I didn't think she'd shoot. If murder was her intent, she could have done it from the cover of the trees around us and then simply helped herself to my coffee, food, and truck. She hadn't, so that told me Miss—or Mrs.—Marcie Rose had something else in mind.

I put the rifle out of mind best I could and went through the motions, trying not to let the tension in my back show too much. The iron skillet got properly arranged next to the coffee pot and the blackened coffee cup got rescued from the coals with a twig and set aside. There was another clean one in the bag. I generally bring along several on the theory that it being just me alone, washing dishes was a low priority item, somewhere below digging a latrine.

I started the bacon to get some grease in the skillet, and then moved them aside and broke half a dozen eggs, stirring with an iron camp spoon. As they began to set, I added in the cheese and the chili. Lots of chili. I liked my scrambled eggs that way and to heck with Miss. Rose's culinary proclivities.

Marcie moved. I made a point of not looking. The truck's door squeaked—I'd have to oil those hinges someday—and a few moments later the engine coughed and sputtered, shaking itself awake after a cold-night's sleep. In a minute the old Ford settled down to a rough idle. I kept my attention strictly on building breakfast. I'd told her she could take it, and if that's what she decided to do, well it was insured. But I didn't think Marcie Rose was ready to leave just yet, at least not until she'd eaten my food too.

She was running from something or someone. No use trying to guess which at this point. It was clear that whatever had driven her out into the cold hadn't been planned. She hadn't dressed for the occasion. A reasonable conclusion would be that Marcie's plunge into the cold was a matter of her seizing an opportunity. Beyond that there was little to gain by speculating. She'd talk in time, if she wanted to.

The eggs hardened and browned and I covered the skillet and moved it off to the side to stay warm.

The truck hadn't moved, and Marcie's tired face looked heavy-eyed past the big steering wheel. I strolled over and opened the door. Her shoes lay in the corner where she'd kicked them off, toes protruding through holes in her hose, nice and pink now, under the heater's fan. The Carcano leaned against the passenger door, replaced by the Smith and Wesson .22 revolver in her lap.

"You found it."

She glanced at the stainless-steel revolver in her hand.

I said, "How long has it been?"

Her view narrowed a little, uncertain.

"Since you last warm meal? Last warm bed? How long have you been wandering around up here nearly barefooted and hiding from your own shadow?"

"I'm not-," She screwed her lips together and straightened up on the seat. "I am not hiding from my shadow, Mister Granger."

"You're running from something."

She frowned out the windshield. There wasn't much to see except Ponderosa pine trees that grow tall on this side of Pikes Peak. The trees half obscured a muddy, double-rutted track I'd driven up on yesterday afternoon.

"Your name really *is* Paul Granger."

I laughed. "Congratulations. You can read vehicle registrations."

She looked at me, half smiled, and leaned wearily on the steering wheel. The barrel of my little revolver remained pointed more or less in my general direction, but now not nearly as steady or with the precision or resolve as had the rifle earlier. The warm cab and her great fatigue had begun to melt the formidable Marcie Rose.

I went around back of the truck, crawled into the aluminum shell and dug out a pair of heavy cotton socks. In a plywood box I located a pair of hiking boots and brushed the dust from them. They were well-worn but sound, and a damn sight more practical than the open-toed sandals she had wandered into camp wearing. Of course, they were about five sizes too large for her, but I didn't think Marcie Rose was much concerned about fashionable ladies' outdoor wear at the moment.

When I appeared at the door again Marcie pushed her head from the steering wheel and peered oddly at me. "Where have you been?" She asked bewildered.

"Here, put these on."

She studied me a long, confused moment, realizing she'd fallen asleep. Her mouth formed word of a question but didn't speak it when she saw the items I was holding. Eyelids narrowing, shading her blue eyes behind a scowl, the revolver gave a little meaningful jerk to show she still meant business and she said, "Just set them on the floor."

"Sure thing, lady. Keep those hungry wolves at bay and all that. Don't let your guard down for a minute." I stepped back a couple paces to reassure her. After all, she did have a gun, and even a little .22 can kill tougher men than me.

She squirmed out from behind the wheel and unrolled the socks. I found a deadfall to sit on to ease her mind. I didn't want her fumbling with a loaded gun while trying to get into something more practical than she was wearing. She set the revolver on the seat beside her, reached under her dress and wiggled out of the shredded pantyhose.

"I have an extra pair of trousers in back if you're interested."

She though it over. "Why not? I already look like a circus clown."

I dug the pants and a spare flannel shirt out of the plywood box and tossed them to her. She stripped off the pastel blue dress that was more mud brown than blue and stood there in bra and panties, shivering, getting the pants oriented. Marcie Rose had a fine figure, easy on the eyes in spite of the grime. She kept one eye on me and the other on the trousers, pulling them quickly up around her waist. Then the shirt. Once the scenery was properly covered up, she moved a little slower, more methodically.

"There wouldn't happen to have an extra belt in the box back there?" she asked buttoning up the fly.

"Sorry. Keeping them up is your problem."

She grinned before she realized what she was doing and instantly removed it from her face. "Well, how about a piece of rope?"

"Rope I can supply." It was at the bottom of the plywood box. By time I came back around the truck Marcie was put back together and lacing up the boots. Her fingers stopped and I saw she was thinking about the gun on the seat. I tossed the rope and pretended not to notice. "Breakfast is waiting. Don't forget to turn off the ignition."

I moved the skillet back over the coals, checked under the lid that nothing had burned, pushed the eggs about with a fork, and poured myself another cup of coffee. I set out two plastic plates—the colorful, unbreakable kind you have around the house when you have little kids—and unfolded a second camp chair.

A wistful glance at the fishing pole and tackle box reminded me of the important business I'd driven up here to transact. Maybe after breakfast. The morning had gotten old, too old for any spectacular angling, but I might be able to coax a late feeder or two to my hook for make lunch...that is if Marcie Rose didn't have other ideas.

CHAPTER 2

The engine stopped, the door squeaked, and footsteps crunched up behind me. I said, "Take a seat and grab a plate."

"Smells good." Marcie moved around where I could see her, lowered herself into the green fabric chair and laid the Carcano on the ground—far side, right-hand side. The revolver was in her pocket. Well, I'd tried to be non-threatening. Maybe it was beginning to occur to her that I really was.

"Well, pick up a plate, Miss Rose," I said when she just sat there. "I cooked it for you, but I'm sure not going to feed you too."

Her lips tightened and she grabbed the yellow one. I scrapped a pile of eggs onto it and half the bacon. "I don't get you, Granger. I could have killed you a half dozen different times. You don't seem to be taking me seriously. You think I'm bluffing?"

"No ma'am, I don't think you're bluffing. What you say is true. You can kill me, take my clothes, eat my food, and steal my truck like you stole that rifle and parka."

Her eyes got narrow. I went on before she could deny it. "But then you'd be all alone again, wouldn't you? That's not what you want or need at the moment, is it?"

She tossed her head and said, "And what do you think I really need, Mr. Psychoanalyst?"

"What you really need is a friend. Someone to help you out of whatever trouble you're in."

She didn't answer, she didn't have to. The softening about her mouth and eyes told me I'd gotten it right.

I filled a coffee cup and handed it to her. "If you kill me, you might just be killing that someone."

She didn't know how to answer that.

"Eat your eggs before they get cold." I carried my green plate to the other green camp chair, set the cup on the ground and balanced the plate on my knee. Breakfast tasted pretty good, with lots of pepper and couple splashes of Tabasco sauce.

"You're a strange man, Granger."

I gave a short laugh. "How's that," I asked around a forkful of scrambled eggs.

From the other side of the campfire she peered at me with tired eyes, an egg-filled fork suspended halfway between her plate and mouth. The corner of her lips tipped down into a small frown. She shook her head, dirty, tangled hair brushing her shoulders. "Not sure. If it had been my campsite and you had steamrolled into it waving a junk rifle, making demands, I'd have been furious. It doesn't seem to bother you."

"It must be my easygoing nature, ma'am." I said offhanded, but my thoughts had taken a turn. Marcie Rose had just told me something important about herself. I don't think she knew she had.

"That's not it."

I shrugged. "What's your theory?"

"Haven't got one...yet."

"Maybe I'm stringing you along until you drop your guard?"

"Maybe. Cockran has connections. One thing is certain. You've had guns pointed at you before."

It was my turn to look surprised.

"It's kind of suspicious finding someone up here in the middle of winter." She nodded at my fishing gear. "Sure, you've got all the right props, but where are the fish? Anyway, who comes up into these mountains in March and freezes their butts just to catch a few lousy fish?" Her eyebrows arched questioningly.

"I do," I said and just learned something else. A man named Cockran was after her.

"Where are they?"

"You a cop?"

She laughed. "Hardly."

"My stomach."

"What?"

"The fish. You asked where they were. I ate them for dinner last night. That is, after all, why I caught them."

"Real convenient."

"And tasty."

Marcie bit the eggs from her fork and stabbed a piece of bacon. "Until I'm certain you don't work for Cockran, I can't take a chance."

"If you say so. More coffee?" She shook her head. I warmed my cup. "So, what does Cockran have on you?"

She looked up sharply. "Can't talk about it."

"That bad?"

"Don't pry."

"Is Cockran the law?"

"No!" She gave me an incredible look. "I told you not to pry."

"You've kind of made it my business to pry."

Marcie swallowed a mouthful of eggs, an unhappy look returning to her face.

I said, "How long have you been wandering around out here?"

"Since yesterday morning."

"Haven't eaten much since, have you?"

"No."

"Give me your plate." I scrapped the remaining eggs from the skillet. She didn't talk and concentrated on eating. I sipped my coffee thinking it over. She still carried a ton of suspicion, but she seemed to have forgotten the revolver in her pocket—well, at least while she took care of her current endeavor of filling the hunger-hole in her stomach. When she'd cleaned the plate, she patted her mouth with the back of her hand and extended the tin cup.

"I'll have some more now, please."

"Please?" I nodded approvingly. "That's a pleasant turn."

Her view narrowed. "Don't get the idea anything has changed. You're still one of the bad guys until I've proven otherwise." The gun reappeared. "I won't hesitate to use this."

I laughed just to show her I wasn't intimidated, although I was a little. In any case, I wasn't ready to call her bluff. "I believe you would. You seem pretty comfortable around firearms, Miss Rose. Where'd you learn to shoot?"

"We had to-," she started to say, and then stopped and scowled into her coffee cup. "I had three brothers. They hunted." She took a drink and stared at me over the cup in her hand. "You're prying again. Put a lid on it."

I stood and went to the fishing gear against a tree.

"Where are you going?" she demanded when I took the rod in hand.

"All of a sudden I have this desire for pleasant company. And since I don't have a dog—supposedly man's best friend—I'll have to settle for the company of the local brook trout."

"You can't just leave now."

"Watch me." I headed for the stream down the hill past a grove of bare-branched aspen trees. Before entering them, I glanced over my shoulder.

Her lips were scrunched, her face tired with a wan, defeated look in her eyes. She had put on a tough act, but the fight had worn her down—that and the weather and the mountains, the grime, and maybe life in general. I suspected a long soak in a warm tub of water would take care of many of her problems—but not all of them. It was easy to feel sorry for her.

I called back, "You're welcome to use the truck heater again. Leave a window cracked. I can't guarantee you won't get carbon monoxide leaking from that rusty exhaust pipe."

"Mr. Granger. Wait."

I stopped while she kicked her way through the winter-brown grass, halting just beyond my reach, her right hand inside the oversized pocket. A man with a fishing rod in one hand and a tackle box in the other wasn't going to suddenly grab her, but she was prepared just in case. Her blue eyes were not threatening now, merely worried.

"I know I've been difficult, but trust me, I really can't tell you what it's all about."

"Lady, I don't trust anyone who points a gun at me."

She grimaced. "You don't know what's involved."

"And it doesn't look like you intend to enlighten me, right?"

"I...I can't." She caught her lower lip in her teeth.

I shot a sleeve and glanced at my watch. "I came up here to go fishing, Miss Rose, and I'm already late getting about business. If I hurry, I just might snag a straggler or two still feeding."

She stared at me and I saw in her face a sudden anger that I had the audacity to be more interested in fish than in her. Well, that wasn't entirely true. I was curious, and pretty sure her problem would prove very interesting, but I'd listen when I was ready to listen. And I wasn't ready yet. I doubted she was going to go anywhere.

I said, "Climb into the truck and get yourself warm again. I'll be back in a while."

"We might not have a while before-." She caught herself again.

"Before what?"

"Oh, never mind," she said irritably and stomped back to camp, hands plunged deep inside those big pockets, head turtled down into the collar.

All of a sudden, I wasn't in the mood to hoof it

down to the stream. I did it anyway because I had told her I was going to. Poking around inside the tackle box produced a fuzzy red and yellow fly that I thought might look tasty to the trout—at least it had yesterday—and cast it out and reeled it back in.

Up the hill the truck's door slammed and the V8 growled awake and settled down to an easy rumbly purr. It didn't drive away. I didn't think it would. I hoped she'd cracked open the window like I'd advised her to do.

I played the line back and forth a while with hardly a nibble, not really paying attention to the business of catching fish. Too many other thoughts had buried that whole enterprise beneath a pile of worry growing inside me. Why the secrecy? Who was Marcie Rose running from? Whatever has frightened her was contagious. Something—a feeling—told me it was time to leave. And who was I kidding anyway, standing here pretending to be catching fish?

I reeled in, gathered up my gear, and glanced at my watch. Seventeen minutes was all. It felt longer. The truck rumbled softly through the trees, idling in its peculiar halfhearted fashion.

She had seemed ready to talk. I wanted to hear what she had to say...or at least was willing to tell me. Trudging up the steep landscape, I tried to piece it together, but so far there wasn't enough to get the corners right let alone the edges.

Coming through the trees, I spied the old beast purring contentedly where I'd left it, but I didn't see Marcie. I set the gear aside, instantly alert. You never forget, not really. You might think you have, but then something unexpected happens and instantly you're back. My reflexes had been dulled somewhat by years in front of a blackboard looking at bored faces using up their GI Bill or burning through mom and dad's bank account. It wasn't the V.C. now, this was a new enemy, and probably just as deadly.

In a glance I surveyed the campsite, seeing nothing out of place. It could be something as innocent as a hike to a distant tree to take care of business, but I wasn't taking any chances. Whatever had frightened Marcie had been very real. I was sure of that.

Had she just up and left on foot? She'd said she couldn't stay. If so, I should feel relief. I didn't. I stayed back among the trees thinking it through. She'd gotten to me with her talk and wild look. I let go of a breath and felt the adrenaline ebb away. I'd lived the dull, safe life for too long. Maybe I was ready to be scared again—just a little—for old time's sake.

Even so, I felt a familiar tingle at the back of my neck as I stepped into the open and approached the truck. It was a feeling I'd learned to depend in another place and another time—another lifetime ago, it seemed, and I was reassured that it was still there, just waiting to be used again.

She'd opened the window a crack like I'd told her to. I peered inside. Stretched out on the seat, an arm for a pillow, knees pulled up in the classic fetal position—which was the only way she could fit on the seat—Marcie Rose slept.

Unlike the driver's door, the passenger's side didn't have the annoying squeak. I quietly opened it, reached across and switched off the ignition. Marcie never stirred as the truck shut down. The air inside was toasty warm.

I eased the rifle from the floorboards, slowly opened the action and ejected the cartridge into my hand. I unloaded the magazine next, putting six more rounds of 6.5 ammo into my pocket. I did the same with the revolver, replacing it gently back near her hand.

Marcie slept like a baby. The air inside the cab would remain reasonably warm now with the sun higher and shining on the faded roof. She'd sleep a while, and she needed it.

I returned to the camp chair by the fire, my pocket heavy with ammunition, the feeling inside me lighter for it. With the remaining coffee now in my cup, I pondered my predicament...and suddenly, for no particular reason I could discern, I thought about Sherri.

CHAPTER 3

The morning had been peaceful. My thoughts were not. Earlier I'd considered brewing another pot of coffee but didn't think we'd be here much longer. The sky to the north was building a bank of low gray clouds, and rain, or maybe snow, threatened. That wasn't the reason why I didn't heat up more water.

I'd tried to ignore it at first, but for the last half hour the far-off baying of hounds had slowly wormed its way into my thoughts. The wind, blowing in from the right direction now, brought that ancient, haunting sound down the mountainside, triggering my early warning system. I grimaced, unable any longer to ignore the klaxon sounding inside my head. Those pups were getting excited, their baying getting louder not softer. They were coming toward me, not away.

If this had been another time, I'd have waited around to see what the dogs were hunting, but Marcie Rose had gotten me psyched out. I had a strong feeling their quarry was the young lady presently asleep inside my pickup truck.

Sound carries a long way down mountain canyons, especially in this cold air, but by the sound of them, those dogs, and whoever was following them, had gotten too close already. I began to fold up camp and haul it to the truck.

When the door squeaked, I poked my head out the camper shell and peered around the side of the truck. "Afternoon, Miss Rose. Have a good nap?"

She looked startled, and then alarmed. "Afternoon?"

"Well, just barely."

"How long have I been asleep?" A note of panic sounded in her voice.

"About three hours, give or take a handful of minutes."

"No. I shouldn't have."

"You fought it off. You needed it."

"You don't understand, Granger. It's not safe for me out here. Or you either."

"Me? I thought I was one of the bad guys. Since when do you worry about the enemy's well-being?"

"Okay. I was wrong." She looked at the revolver in her hand, at her side. "I probably wouldn't still have this if you were."

"Probably not," I said sharply.

"I don't blame you for being mad."

I scooted out of the camper and gathered up the cardboard box of groceries.

She said, "When I came upon your camp this morning I almost crept past it, but the smell of coffee, and a fire...Guess I barged in on your life like a linebacker for the Broncos, didn't I?"

"If that's an apology, I accept it." The sleeping bag

and fishing gear got tossed in behind the food.

She watched me. "Ruined your fishing trip?"

"Yes ma'am, you did a fine job of that."

She looked back at the clearing, and then me, finally putting it together. "You're leaving?"

"We're leaving. As you've noted, the trip has been ruined."

All at once her head snapped around and the gun came up from her side. "What's that?"

That, Miss Rose, is a dog—well, a couple dogs. Bloodhound by the sound of it."

I didn't think a pair of eyes could open that wide. I said, "They've been moving around out there about twenty minutes now. Getting closer. You wouldn't know anything about that, would you?"

"Ted Bant had a couple dogs." There was a sudden tightness in her throat. "They're on me. We have to get out of her," she said.

"Might only be a couple pooches running down rabbits."

Her view shot back at me. "You know that's not it."

"I don't know that, but I'm not going to take any chances. Get in the truck. I'm almost done here."

Marcie hesitated, then got into the passenger side. I broke up the coals and did a quick scan of the site. If someone really was after her, I didn't want anything lying around that might lead them to me. I was climbing up behind the wheel when those dogs howled, this time so close I looked over my shoulder to make sure a pooch hadn't jumped into the camper. "They're closer than I thought," I said shoving the shifter into second gear—first gear is granny low and practically worthless for anything but pulling tree stumps. The mud and snow tires kicked up and tail of dirt behind and I cranked the steering wheel hard sending the old truck into a two-wheel drift that got her pointing the right direction down the rutted track I'd come up yesterday.

Two dogs appeared in the mirror. They bounded from the trees into the clearing, put their noses to the ground, ran a couple circles, then let out mournful bays and lunged after the truck and for a few seconds nipped at its tires. We pulled away from them, but not before three men appeared at the edge of the clearing. One of them threw a rifle to his shoulder.

Crack. Thud.

And then the trail curved and I lost them in the mirror.

Marcie cast an angry glance at me. "They saw us—saw your truck. Dammit, Granger. Dammit all to hell!"

They saw an old pickup truck that looks like a thousand others in this part of the country. I was pretty sure they hadn't got the license number. Hadn't been enough time. I didn't tell her that. I had more important matters at the moment to occupy my thoughts. It was like riding in a Mixmaster. We bounced as swayed down that mountain track, crashed into washouts, flew over high spots. Those dogs were still there but losing ground. Marcie had an arm over the back of the seat, bracing her other hand on the dash, teeth chattering and stringy hair whipping.

The track straightened some and widened a little to where it might be called a road...if you were being generous with your terminology. We'd left the dogs behind. I let up on the gas a little and the ride calmed a bit. At least we weren't fighting to keep from cata-pulting through the windshield. I said, "All they saw was a rust-red 1950-something Ford pickup truck. No way anyone will be able to trace it."

Marcie looked skeptical. "It wears a camper. They might have seen your plate."

"If they can read that bent-up thing, Superman's got nothing over them. Someday that plate will earn me a ticket. As far as the camper goes, eight bolts takes it off." I grinned to show I wasn't concerned. I'm not sure that was to reassure her or me.

Marcie didn't look convinced by my logic. I said, "Hey, they're behind us and on foot. Unless they have a radio and call ahead for reinforcements to meet us at the highway, we're practically home free."

Her narrow view slid my way, still not convinced.

I said, "We'll get out of these mountains and find us a nice restaurant someplace. You'll feel better after a real meal, not my camp cooking." I thought I'd made a good argument, but it hadn't fooled her— hadn't fooled me either.

Millin's Timber Inn was located just outside the mountain village of Woodland Park, set off the highway in tall pines. It was a quaint little restaurant housed in a log building that over the years had seen too many coats of white paint. I'd often wondered when I'd driven past the place, which had been pret-ty frequently here lately, why anyone would paint a charming log building. Recently, lodge-type homes have become fashionable—or at least come back into fashion—and if painted at all, the color was usually in a nice forest brown. Mostly, they're left a natural hue, and that's the way I preferred them.

The gravel parking lot was nearly empty. I pulled up near the door, set the parking brake so that the truck wouldn't roll back onto highway 24, and switched off the headlights.

Inside the doorway, Marcie veered off toward the ladies room calling a bar order to me while I stood by an abandoned cash register in obedience to a sign requesting me to do so until officially greeted and escorted through the roomful of mostly empty tables to the one table that was meant for me.

I waited, hands thrust into my pockets, looking out a tall window at the darkening parking lot. Not counting my truck, there were three other vehicles there. I glance over at tables. Only two of them appeared occupied. Turning back, the window darkly mirrored a scruffy face. I rubbed the bristles at my chin. These last few months I'd not been very religious about shaving. My own little rebellion of sorts, I mused and grinned at the reflection grinning back at me.

An attractive greeter-type person arrived to collect me just then. She wore a Bavarian holiday costume like you see at an Octoberfest. "One?" she asked.

"Two," I said holding up the appropriate number of digits.

She snatched a pair of menus from behind the counter and guided me into the larger room with dimmed ceiling lights. I ordered the drinks. The bartender was fast and they arrived before Marcie returned from what I suspected was some serious scrubbing and rearranging.

The costumed waitress went off to tend to the other guests. In one corner a lady and her gentleman friend leaned close over tall drinks, their table cluttered with dirty dishes. They didn't seem to notice. Miss Bavaria was presently catering a table of four across the room. Loud chattering came from that direction. The rest of the place was empty. Behind me stretched a long, white wall hung with some very old-looking photographs of steam engines and long passenger trains crossing spindly, timber trestles.

Marcie came into the room, glanced around, and spied me at the table. I'd already worked halfway through my Glenlivet when she slid into the chair across from me and took a long, passionate drink from the White Russian waiting for her.

"Whew," she said finally, licking the creamy white residue from her upper lip. "I feel half human again. I think I rinsed half of the Rocky Mountains down the drain."

"Welcome back to the human race." I grinned, admiring the face across the table. Some women have God's cosmetic kit built into their genes, the right skin tone, just the right pink tint to their lips, a little more black in their brows.

She returned the comb I'd lent her on the drive down from the pass. "Thanks." And then she said again, "My comb and everything else was in my purse, and who knows where that is now."

"I bet you have a good idea, though."

Her lips tightened. "None I care to discuss—at

least not on an empty stomach," she said mat-ter-of-factly and lowered her view to the glass of scotch on the little white napkin. "You've a head start on me, Granger."

"I didn't know we were racing."

She took another sip and glanced about the restaurant. "Not many people. Good. Not sure I'm ready for crowds just yet." She surveyed her clothes with a disdainful eye. "You don't happen to have any cigarettes?"

"Sorry, don't smoke."

"I shouldn't either, but then I do a lot of things I shouldn't." She unfolded the menu and studied it a moment, then closed it and laid it back on the table. "They took everything, even my credit card, but I can pay you back when we get down to the Springs."

I nodded at the lump in the coat pocket she'd worn in and set on the chair next to her. "That goes for the revolver too?"

She leaned suddenly forward and said, "Not too loud. It's illegal in this state to carry a concealed gun." The ardor in her whispered words made me uncertain that she wasn't just joking.

She scowled at me. "What's that look for?"

I said, "Judging from your behavior this morning I wouldn't have thought such things would concern you."

She leaned back in the chair. "Don't jump to any conclusions about me, Granger. I happen to have a healthy respect for the law, especially in my position—" she stopped, her frown deepening.

"And what position would that be?"

"Think you're pretty clever, huh?" She looked annoyed. "If you must know, I am a secretary."

She left that dangling like a carrot. I said, "Okay, I'll bite. What does being a secretary have to do with your sterling respect for the law?" I took a sip of Glenlivet, watching her over the rim of the glass as she considered her answer.

She raked her lower lip with her teeth and said, "My job requires a security clearance and even something as little as a misdemeanor might jeopardize that. So, let's drop it for now."

I said, "Let's not." I was feeling clever, which usually is a silly if not dangerous notion. "I happen to know something about security clearances and being a secretary with one has little to do with you being familiar with the local firearm laws."

Marcie gave me a pitiful eye look and shook her head. "Really, Granger, you're becoming tiresome."

"Answer the question, Miss. Rose."

The sigh she gave was heavy with theatrical exasperation. "You think you've got me?"

"I think so."

"I can read. You know, newspapers, magazines, newsletters."

Have you ever run across a person who always had a quick answer for everything? I had the feeling that Marcie Rose was one of those kinds. I shrugged. "Reading is a useful skill for a secretary to possess."

She smiled. "Don't worry about your gun," her voice lowered to a whisper on that last word. "—It'll be returned soon as we get down to the Springs."

She paused when our Bavarian waitress appeared, order pad and pencil in hand. We ordered and when Miss Bavaria departed Marcie said, "Now that you know all there is to know about me, how about you?" I detected a hint of playful mockery in her voice. "Are you on vacation?"

I'd hardly learned anything from Marcie. She was telling me to back off and stop being nosy. Well, it was her business, and although her business had now become my business, I let the remark pass. "I guess you can call it a vacation, a very long vacation."

A glimmer of concern came to her otherwise guarded eyes. "You're out of work?"

I laughed. "Only temporarily. It's called a sabbatical."

Concern turned to interest. "You're a teacher?"

"Does that surprise you?"

"I wouldn't have guessed. What do you teach?"

"Freshmen, sophomores, juniors, and seniors...a few graduate students, although not necessarily in that order."

She smiled. "Does this mean I have to call you Doctor Granger now?"

"Not unless you become one of my students." I signaled Miss Bavaria with my raised glass. She held up two fingers. I nodded and she trotted off in the direction of the bar. "Actually, I teach biology, when I'm not off doing my own research."

"Is that what you're doing now? Research?"

"It was my good intentions. It's what the university assumes I'm doing. Fishing, however, has intruded a bit on good intentions." I grinned. "My brother owns a cabin west of here near Florissant. He gave me the keys and I came up about a month ago."

"From where?"

"Portales."

"Where's that?"

"It's a little eastern New Mexico town. Mostly agricultural. Noted primarily for growing peanuts. There's a sign on the highway as you drive into Portales from Clovis proclaiming the place to be the *Peanut Basin of the Nation.* A dubious distinction, don't you think? Peanuts and Eastern New Mexico University are the primary industries there. I believe the students make up at least half the local population."

She laughed, her eyes crinkling in a cute, pixie smile. A pleasant change from the severe, wary side she'd shown up until now. "It sounds like a wonderfully safe life."

I frowned and peered at the empty glass in my hand. "A safe life is what I was looking for."

"Are those the sober words of a man whose past is too terrible to remember?" There was a hint of melodrama in her voice.

"I wouldn't call it terrible," I said seriously, "but it certainly wasn't any fun either. Well, in the beginning maybe, when I wasn't being scared. The planning was fun, and then coming back alive was usually a cause for celebration. Towards the end..." I shook my head, "...it wasn't fun at all. We just wanted to finish the job and come home, as far away from a jungle as we could get."

"Vietnam?"

"Me and a several thousand other men."

She narrowed her view as if trying to gather to a deeper meaning from my words. "Why is it I get the feeling you weren't soldiering like most of those thousands?"

I studied her a moment and then made a smirk to lighten the suddenly heavy mood. "Well, I have no idea why you have that feeling, Miss. Rose. Too fertile imagination maybe? An overactive pituitary gland?"

Marcie leaned her head to one side. "Is that your diagnosis, doctor?"

"Best I can offer right now."

"I get the picture. It's something you'd rather not talk about."

"Now we both have a secret, don't we?"

Her expression tightened slightly. "Subject officially dropped. So, how do you manage when you're away from work? Do you get paid for being on sabbatical, ahem, researching?"

"Money? Paid? Ha. You see what I'm driving."

"You were willing to give the truck away not long ago," she reminded me.

"You recall the rate of exchange?"

"Your life? Did you really think I intended to put a bullet through that broad forehead of yours and get blood all over that nice-looking hair?"

"In a word. Yes."

Marcie Rose stopped smiling and took a sip of her drink. She'd lost the light mood of a moment ago. "Let's talk about something else."

"We can talk about attractive secretaries who run around cold Colorado mountains in March wearing nothing but light, office-type clothes and open toed sandals, being pursued by dangerous gents with rifles."

"That's not a good subject either," she said flatly, drawing back into her moody cocoon.

CHAPTER 4

Our second round of drinks and the food arrived simultaneously and the conversation changed directions as we arranged napkins, rattled silverware, and got down to the pressing business of filling the empty hole in our midsections. We worked diligently at the job, politely refraining from demonstrating to the few patrons seated about the room how wolfishly hungry we really were.

By time I'd sopped up the last of the gravy with my remaining scrap of French bread, Marcie was signaling for her third White Russian. I've encountered the concoction once or twice. Personally, they are too sweet for my liking. It's a sneaky drink. The cream acts as a buffering agent, hiding the alcohol in the vodka and Kahlua while they crept up behind you with a cudgel. When you're tired, and relaxed, as Marcie appeared to be now, it's easy to sneak past the brain's forward guard and scramble a few brain cells.

Miss Bavaria brought over Marcie's drink and turned an inquiring eye toward me. I shook my head and put a palm over the rim of the glass. "I'm driving. But I will have some coffee."

Marcie said, "I like a man who knows when to stop, who doesn't feel it's macho to keep up with the lady." I wasn't sure if I'd been insulted or complimented. "You won't mind if I indulge myself tonight. I've had a bad week."

"Go ahead. Indulge."

She smiled. "And thank you Mister, err, I mean Doctor Granger." She was already pretty loose. "Carl always knew when he'd had enough too..." That had been unintentional. When she realized what she'd said she shut her mouth, letting her smile slip. She stared gloomily into her glass, tilting it sideways watching the remains of her drink sag thickly around the inside rim.

I finished my whiskey. Marcie appeared to be off somewhere, brooding. After a while her blue eyes lifted and peered at me. I had a feeling I wasn't coming in quite in focus.

I said, "Who's Carl?"

Her head gave a single shake, her eyes heavy. "Just someone I used to know." The finality in that was hard to mistake.

"How did he die?"

"I never said he died."

"You didn't have to say the words."

She scowled and the irritation in her voice rose nicely, but not very convincingly. "You teach psychology too? If you must know, he was killed."

"An accident?" Talking about it seemed hard for her, but I had the feeling this was something she wanted to tell me—had probably been thinking all evening how to broach it. Maybe it was the reason for her ambitious drinking now? Her dilemma was, it was something she knew she ought to be keeping to herself.

She gave a short, bitter laugh. "No accident, Granger."

"How long ago?"

Marcie bit her lip and pondered the empty glass she rolled between her palms. "Two weeks."

Miss Bavaria arrived with Marcie's White Russian and my coffee and asked if we wanted dessert. I said no, and she left a bill on a shiny metal tray, collected the dirty dishes, and headed back to the kitchen. Marcie took a drink.

I said, "Do you know who did it?"

"I know who drove the car that killed Carl, or at least I know it was one of three possible men. But they were following orders. The one who gave the order...well, I have a good idea who that might be."

"Hold up. Suppose you shift into reverse."

"You mean you want background?" She looked amused.

"Those three men we just missed getting acquainted to this afternoon. Were they the three who killed your Carl?"

"He wasn't *my* Carl," she snapped, the alcohol getting to her. Someone at the table across the way looked over. Marcie lowered her voice. "And no. I mean no, not completely. Two of them, they might be anyone. The third, the guy in the plaid shirt—"

"The one with the rifle?"

She nodded. "That's right. He was one of the three,

but I'm sure the other two with him are capable of murder. They just weren't the ones."

I was a little confused. I think she was too. Her drink of choice was pretty potent, and she was working on the third one. "What about the other two who were involved in Carl's death.

"*Death* is too sanitized a word for it, Granger. Carl was murdered."

The fellow at the table glanced over again. Marcie grimaced, her Audrey Hepburn-ish jaw taking a hard set. "I don't think I should be telling you this."

"Probably not. Let's get out of here before someone pulls up a chair and joins us. There's at least one pair of ears bent our way. Where is it you said you lived?"

"Wait a minute." Her hand came down on my arm and her voice lowered. "There's too much at stake. I have to be careful. You can understand that, can't you?" She was trying to sound reasonable, but she was plainly drunk and having trouble pronouncing her words. I believed her. There was something big here at stake, and the bullet that had put a hole in the tailgate of my truck had been very real.

I said, "I'll deliver you to whatever address you say. I'll forget about this morning and everything you've told me, which hasn't been much, and tomorrow I'll scout out another fishing hole. Preferably one far away from mysterious females running around in the wilderness practically barefooted and pointing rifles at harmless strangers." I started to stand.

She put pressure on my arm. "All right. I'll talk. But youse gots to promise not to tell any-, anyone, person, people."

I said, "Should I hold up three fingers and say 'scout's honor'?"

She pushed out her lower lip and giggled. "That's right out of Saturday morning cartoon shows."

"You're getting corny, Marcie, or drunk."

"I prefer to think it's the liquor. All right. The second of the tree was at the cabin. Don't knows where turd the man was."

"Turd man?" I untangled her sentence and said, "This is getting confusing. Maybe they have names? If you don't want to tell me that, we can give them each a letter like A, B, and C."

"I got names. Firsts, no lasts.. The man in the lumberjack shirt, he's Alexander. Another, he Jeff. Jeff is a real grade-A asshole creep. Checks his wavy hair ever window mirror he passes. Puts hands place they no belong." Marcie took another drink.

"I'm going to have to carry you out of here if you don't ease off," I warned.

She ignored me. "Th-th-third man I see only at a distance. Thin, kinda austere looking. Probably spend his childhood looking at insects through a magnifying glass. Raymond him...err...his name."

"Interesting collection," I said. "What about Carl. If he wasn't *your* Carl, who was he?"

"We were friends...close friends." She lowered her head slightly and peered up at me in a meaningful way.

"I see. You were close, but not close enough to claim possession."

Marcie looked at the drink on the table, in her hand. "He had a wife."

"One of those complicated triangles," I said.

"Complicated. Yes, I guess you could call it that. Anyway, his wife is not a part of this."

"Except to the extent that she is now a widow."

Marcie winced.

I said, "There was another name. Cockran." I sipped my coffee.

Marcie shivered. "What can I tell you about Cockran," she said, making it a statement not a question. "Earlier I say didn't know who give…gave the order to kill Carl but suspected who did it. Sten Cockran, he gives the orders. What I don't know is who Cockran takes his orders from."

"Cockran is only a link in a chain?"

"Everyone a chain in a link, got someone over them," she said unhappily. "He take him orders and like it, or he ends up in a cold hole. Simple that."

"Sounds like the company he works for has a pretty good solution to any underfunded retirement program they might have."

Miss Bavaria swept by and collected the metal tray with my cash.

"How do you know these people?" I asked when we were alone again.

"Work. Sort of. I knows Carl from work, and Cockran too. Him three goons I only see oc…occ… occasionally, lapping their master heels."

"Doesn't sound like a fun place of employment."

She sighed. "Honestly, I had no idea what I was get into when I take job at STE. Space Technologies Electronics," she explained. "In hindsight, I should stayed at that frumpy real estate office with its frumpy gray-suits-and-ties salesmen. It might have been boring work but at least when someone died, it was from natural causes. And they didn't wear suits with bulges under their arms either."

A thought nudged my brain and I peered past Marcie trying to remember what it was. "What?" she asked frowning. "Haven't you seen a woman ever drown her sorrows in booze?"

"I'm trying to remember."

"What? The last time you see a drunk?"

"If I knew, I wouldn't be trying to remember it." I grinned. "Space Technologies Electronics...Something in the papers recently, or maybe on TV?"

Marcie laughed drunkenly. "You mean that circus with all those peace freaks marching with their self-righteous signs. A regular three-ringer. Even our illustrious state senator took to the soapbox next to that loudmouth Baptist minister. Those pulpit thumpers cryin' for peace at all costs turn my stomach."

My thoughts were elsewhere as she called down fire on the whole peace movement, damning the Soviet Union and Gorbachev. When she came up for air, I said calmly, "Something about nuclear warheads and a government contract to build them." I noticed that the table across the way was empty, and that was a good thing as Marcie's words had gotten heated.

"Not whole warhead, Ga-Granger" she said impatiently. "Just the electronic detonator. Been redesigned, more sopohisticated, more sensivative, and STE developed them. The government give STE contract to manufacture the RD-35s to retrofit the ICBM arsenal. That's why those peaceniks swarmed the parking lot like ants at a picnic."

"Interesting."

"That's an understatement. These people didn't organize all on their own. You...you realize how much
money involve here, Granger? Special interest groups
have their fingerprints all over the demonstrations."
Her view narrowed suddenly. "You aren't a peacenik,
are you?" The topic seemed to have sobered her.

I wasn't sure what Marcie's definition of Peacenik
was, however, I did understand what war was. It was
no fun, and something I wanted nothing to do with.
I said, "There are lots of ways to die, Miss Rose, few
of them good, especially on a battlefield. These days
I try to remain neutral where religion, politics, and
national defense are concerned."

"That's a cop-out."

Miss Bavaria arrived with a tray full of change,
two candy mints, and a *Thank You, Dora* scribbled
on the receipt. Dora invited us to come back soon
and drifted off across the empty restaurant floor.

"Shall we continue this discussion in the truck?"

"Cutting me off already?" Marcie guzzled the rest
of her drink. "I better run to the lady's room again if
I'm going to spend another hour bouncing around
in that old truck of yours." She attempted to set her
glass back on the table, missed and hit the edge of
the metal tray. The coins flew out, wobbled across
the table, and thumped onto the carpet.

"Damn, Granger, I think I'm tipsy." She looked
around the room, embarrassed. Fortunately, we
were alone. Marcie got down and began gathering
the coins. I helped. "This is all I can find," she said
dumping two pennies and a nickel onto the tray.

"Don't worry about it," I said, "sure you can make it the little girls' room on your own?"

"You offering to hold my hand?" Her brows arched questioningly. "I'm a big girl. I won't fall in." She stood unsteadily and steered a zigzagging path through the tables toward the hall, and the restrooms around the corner. I watched her reflection in the tall window. Once out of sight her manner of walking improved dramatically. She passed the door with the skirted stick figure...and out of the range of the window's reflection.

She staggered back into the eating area two minutes later, swaying a bit. She gripped the back of her chair to steady herself. "Ready."

"Feel better?"

"Should be good for the trip home." She gave a lopsided smile.

"Let's get going then." I took her arm in a show of concern and aimed her toward the door. As we made our way outside, I glanced over toward the restrooms and the pay phone on the wall there. Its long, coiled cord was still gently turning ever decreasing circles.

CHAPTER 5

My breath hung in the cold air as I zipped my coat, took Marcie's arm, and started for the truck. All at once Marcie stiffened and held back. Even half drunk, she was alert—more so than me and I was sober.

"What?" I asked, glancing around the dark parking lot.

Her reply was a whisper. "Someone in the shadows, other side of your truck," and then she added loudly, "Damn! I left my lighter on the table. I'll be right back," she spun on her heels and dashed back into the restaurant.

Whatever she'd seen, I'd missed it. Maybe it was only a mountain ghost from the past? Marcie was already halfway across the eating area by time I caught up with her and grabbed her arm. She turned on me, rattlesnake quick, a wild look in her eyes.

"What?" I asked again.

"You didn't see him?" Neither one of us cared who heard us.

"See who?"

"You weren't looking, Granger. There's got to be

a back door to this place." Marcie yanked her arm from my grasp and pushed through a swinging door into brightly lit kitchen.

A rotund cook in a dingy apron looked up from a grill he'd been scrubbing. "Hey, you can't come in here."

"Where's the back door," she demanded, cutting him short.

"I told you. You can-"

The revolver suddenly in Marcie's hand caused the man to gulp back his words. "The *door!*"

"O-o-over there, lady." A plump finger pointed down a dim hallway.

"I grimaced, gave the man an apologetic grin and followed Marcie. She paused at the door and gave me a worried glance. She cracked the door and peered outside.

"Don't see them here," she whispered, clear relief in her voice.

I said, "Did you really see something out in the parking lot?"

Her view narrowed angrily. "I'm not that drunk, Granger. I didn't imagine at least two pairs of feet by the back corner of the truck."

"If you're right, what are you planning to do about it?" I'm not sure I wanted to hear the answer to that, but I was too involved to back out now.

"Get far away from here."

That didn't sound like much of a plan. "On foot? It's cold out there."

"You don't like it, go back to your truck and see for yourself. Let them work you over for a couple hours. See how you like it."

I ignored the anger. "They'll be getting suspicious about now. It doesn't take five minutes to retrieve a lighter." I looked out the door, along the dark backside of the building, then took her wrist and hauled her after me. I sensed she didn't approve of the sudden change in command, but she was smart enough to know this was not the time or place to argue the point.

It was darker back here, with a few scattered lights from Woodland Park showing through the trees. We made for those lights.

A husky voice from beyond the corner of the building shouted, "There they are!"

Two black silhouettes appeared in the glow of the parking lot lights. I tugged Marcie toward a dark stand of trees. They closed behind us as we plunged through the forest, seeing our way by the faint moonlight pushing through the treetops. We stumbled over unseen rocks, caught our feet on deadfall branches, making our way deeper into the woods.

I had no sense of how far we'd gone. Crashing around in the dark distorts time and distance. What felt like a quarter mile might easily be only a few hundred yards. But at least we were on equal terms with the two men somewhere behind us; they couldn't see any better than we could.

I stopped abruptly and went to my haunches, pulling Marcie down low with me. She was breathing hard. I was too.

"What?" she asked.

"Quiet," I whispered, straining to hear past the pounding of blood in my ears.

"They're still out there," she whispered. "I hear

them talking back and forth."

"Yeah. I hear them too." I looked at her. "Someone must want you pretty bad."

"It's us now, Granger. Someone wants us pretty bad," she whispered.

I gave a wry smile, which I don't think she could see. "How did a harmless fishing trip turn into a cat and mouse game like this?"

"I know how these people think. If they catch up with us now it won't be a simple drive to an isolated mountain cabin and not-so-friendly questions and answers. It will be the big send off this time." She pointed a finger on her head and snapped her thumb down in a meaningful way. "Tomorrow or the next someone will find two frozen bodies."

"Maybe." My thoughts were somewhere else, somewhere a lot warmer and just as dangerous. That once-familiar tightness filled my chest again, sharpened my senses, focused my thoughts.

The revolver was back in Marcie's hand.

I said softly, "There's two of 'em out there somewhere. You shoot at one, you better get both or you'll give away your position."

"Okay. We take them out quietly, one by one." A bit of sarcasm came to her voice. "You wouldn't happen to have a big knife handy."

I glanced at her. "You're a bloodthirsty woman, aren't you?"

"I'm a pragmatist. The fact is, we can't spend all night playing hide and seek."

"I don't intend to. Ever do any night hunting?"

"It's illegal," she reminded me.

"Geeze lady, you sure you're not a cop?"

She glared at me.

I said, "Stay close and try not to make like a herd of buffalo...well, bison if you want to get technical."

"Spare me the biology lesson, Professor Granger. What's the plan?"

"Let see if we can create a diversion, to get a bead on their location, and then work our way up behind them."

"I hope you know what you're doing."

I did too. They were getting closer, their soft back and forth talk clearer now. They weren't trying to be sneaky.

"See anything?"

"Naw, they're gone...or gone to ground."

Twigs snapped.

"Keep looking."

"It's cold out here."

Working out a rough triangulation on their voices, I leaned to Marcie's ear and whispered, "You get to be the rabbit."

"Thanks. Which way does this bunny run?"

I pointed. "As fast as you can without tripping or crashing into a tree. Keep low. When a person shoots blindly, they tend to aim high. Hopefully you won't give them anything more solid to shoot at than some sound."

"Hopefully?" I heard a genuine lack of enthusiasm in her voice.

The crunch of their footsteps was drawing nearer, an occasional word between them sketching their location pretty clearly in my brain. I felt the ground and found a stone that fit nicely in my hand. "When I give the word," I whispered.

A rock was a pretty poor match for a gun, but it was quiet, and didn't give off a muzzle flash.

"Ready?"

Marcie nodded.

Nearby shapeless shadows moved.

"Ready...ready...ready..." I whispered as a sort of mental pacing. Marcie picked up on it. I was aware of her tensing.

One of the shadows took on form.

"Now."

Marcie sprung to the left. I moved right at the same instant and glimpsed her vague shape darting away, hunched over. A gunshot rang out and a bright orange muzzle flash pinpointed the shooter. He fired again. The blast covered the sound of my leap. I came up behind him and swung the rock into his skull. He went down hard and stayed down.

Only in movies does the good guy clobber the bad guy, and then runs off without availing himself to the bad guy's gun. In this case it was a compact automatic with checkered grips. That was about all I could determine in the dark. I guessed it to be a nine-millimeter, or .380. That's the usual caliber for automatics of this diminutive size. I'd already determined it was larger than a .22 from the muzzle blast.

"Walt! Walt!" A rising note of concern marked the second man's voice as he crashed toward us in the dark. His heavy form took shape, drew to a halt, and bent over near enough for me to hear labored breathing. Running plainly was not an activity he did often.

He straightened. "Walt, where are you?" He swung about, waving a pistol carelessly as he came forward again. Something moved in the dark, close by. He saw it and wheeled about. "Walt?"

Something like an explosion of arms and legs burst from the shadows. What followed in the next three or four seconds happened so fast that by the time it took me to realize I wasn't watching a Bruce Lee movie being acted out here in a cold Colorado forest, it was all over.

Marcie had thrown at least a dozen fancy chops and jabs. An expertly placed snap of a foot into his chest had sent him flying backwards, landing in the dark somewhere. He'd gave a single groan, and then went silent.

She slowly eased from what a frozen stance that couldn't have been comfortable to hold. I came up beside her—slowly so that she'd properly identify me—peered down at the crumpled shape. "Remind me to be at my gentlemanly best around you, Miss Rose."

She turned her head toward me, the wild—the same look I'd seen earlier this morning when she'd come into my campsite. "The other one?" she asked in a strictly business-like voice.

"Dead. Or he ought to be. If not, we probably should get him to a hospital." I grimaced. "I hope there's a really good reason for what we did here tonight. One good enough to keep both of us out of jail."

She studied me a long moment trying to make up her mind. "This is hardly the place to discuss it, Granger. We need to find somewhere safe. Then we can talk."

I managed a halfhearted grin. "My cabin...or yours? Yours is likely being watched with more eyes than a bee."

"Bee?"

"Never mind. It's a biological metaphor."

CHAPTER 6

"A gathering of vultures," Marcie said.

There was no emotion attached to that, only a calculating undertone that made me very uneasy. We were hunkered on a low ridge above the Timber Inn Restaurant. From our position the land fell steeply away to the lighted parking lot below. Behind us it climbed at a frightening angle into black nothingness.

A swarm of men milled about the lighted lot, some peering into the cab of my parked truck. Others investigating along the backside of the restaurant. A couple just standing there looking cold and un-interested. More cars arrived. I counted eight men all together.

Marcie studied the situation, a pout pressed into her lips.

I said, "Scratch the truck. We'll have to walk."

She didn't answer. Her pout remained. I got the feeling it wasn't disappointment, or even despair, but the outward display of a mind wholly occupied plotting its next move.

And then it struck me what that next move was, that she was presently so carefully pondering. I said, "If you're thinking what I think you're thinking you can count me out. I feel obliged to tell you suicide is not on my list of fun things to do."

She pulled her view off the busy scene below and narrowed it at me. "We're both armed now. If we hit them by surprise-"

"Geeze, lady. The bodies are really piling up, and I have no intention of personally adding to the number, thank you very much. By my count there are eight men down there and who knows how many more might be showing up. You're armed with an anemic little twenty-two, and I have a three-eighty with four rounds in the magazine and one in the chamber. A pistol, I might remind you, which I've never fired. Your six and my five leave little margin for error." I didn't mention that she was carrying an unloaded revolver. "We're outnumbered, outgunned, and you want to reenact the final scene from *Butch Cassidy and the Sundance Kid!* Forget it!"

Her expression reminded me of carved ice, but she couldn't hold it. The corners of her lips crept upward, and she struggled to contain a low laugh. "You really do think I'm a bloodthirsty wench."

I shrugged, a little relieved as the tension drained from her face. "You didn't exactly play patty cake with that gent back there.

"Don't worry, Granger, I'll keep an eye on that *precious hide* of yours. And I'm not plagued with suicidal tendencies either."

"Then I suggest we slip quietly away from here

before your friends get the clever notion to beat the bushes hunting for my precious hide, and yours."

"Slip quietly away to where?"

"I really don't care at the moment."

"Look." She pointed. "That man coming out of the restaurant, that's Alexander."

"The one who put a bullet hole in my tailgate?"

"In the flesh."

"What about that other one, Jeff?"

Marcie frowned. "I don't see ol' roaming hands among them."

"Cockran?"

"Hahaha. Cockran doesn't get his hands dirty in public. He has underlings to do that."

Two men emerged from the shadows behind the building. Between them they supported a limp shape, either Marcie's or the one I took out. The man was alive, his legs trying to keep up, but not doing a very good job at it.

Marcie said, "They've been found."

"This seems the appropriate time to get out of Dodge, wouldn't you say?"

"Another minute..."

I couldn't see any profit in hanging around but just then a pickup truck turned off the highway into the lot and stopped alongside my old rig, its new paint reflecting the overhead lights. Mine looked dull and worn-out beside it. Two stout, four-footed critters jumped out of the bed, metronome tails beating a prestissimo tempo, making happy romps around the men there as if each one needed a wet tongue greeting. "Oh no. Bant and his hounds."

Marcie's wide eyes turned toward me. "Yes, I believe getting out of Dodge would be a good idea."

We moved away from our vantage point, scrambled up the rising land, found a gully that pointed us away from the activity around the restaurant, and ended on a deer trail up the mountainside.

Between heavy breaths and mild cussing, Marcie said, "You have any idea where we're heading?"

"Of course not." Just because she'd found me camping in the mountains didn't mean I knew about every obscure trail like the old Ute Indians that used to inhabit these parts. Maybe I should have been flattered by her confidence in me? I gave her a hand over a fallen tree across the path.

"Was afraid of that," she said unhappily.

We worked our way up the steep landscape and came to a gravel road only slightly brighter than the forested gloom we'd emerged from, running off into blackness both directions.

She peered up one direction and down the other. "Which way?"

"Can't see as it makes much difference." I studied it a moment. "Unless I'm completely turned around, that direction is away from Woodland Park." The trees were too thick to see any village lights, so I was guessing.

"Then that's the way we'll go."

"Yes ma'am."

"Maybe we'll come to a house?" she wondered.

"Maybe," I agreed. It wasn't much of a conversation and I was glad when it ended making it easier to listen for the muffled growl of tires on gravel, or the baying of hunting hounds. All I heard was the soft crunch of our footsteps.

I let Marcie have the lead, and she seemed happy to take it. We marched on, my senses on high alert, sifting sounds and expecting any moment to see headlights reflecting in the distance...thinking, ruefully, of all those fish I could be pulling out of a safe, friendly stream if a certain Miss Rose hadn't stumbled into my life.

I glanced at the luminescent hands of my wristwatch. It wouldn't take long for the hounds to find our trail. So far, I hadn't heard anything.

Marcie stopped abruptly. I walked into her and grabbed a handful of her parka to stop her from falling.

"Watch where you're going." She shook me off.

"You need to get that brake light fixed."

"Shush! I hear something. Over that way." She pointed.

I heard it too. Softly, from the darkness came the unmistakable beat of rock and roll music. Not loud as Rock ought to be played—or endured as the case may be—but muted by trees and distance. We looked at each other, reading each other's thoughts. Advancing along the road, the noise growing.

A narrow, two-rut track angled off the road, cutting back into the trees. The noise got louder; a voice crying *It's a heartache, nothing but a heartache,* accompanied ample orchestration. Someone's *heartache* was rapidly becoming my earache. The double ruts ended in a clearing a few hundred feet off the road where a compact station wagon sat.

It was one of those tiny Japanese imports I was seeing a lot of. They'd become fashionable over here ever since the oil embargo of a few years back. In the dark it was impossible to tell the color. Its windows appeared steamed over and from within came the pale green glow from the radio. The music poured from a partly opened driver's side window. Past the blare of it, the car's engine purred softly, but I didn't see anyone sitting behind the wheel. There was something else odd about the way the car rocked on its springs.

In the dark I glimpsed Marcie's mischievous smile. "It alive." Her voice was low, breathless. It was plain she'd been doing some breath-holding only a moment before. Well, I had done a little of that myself.

I said, "It seems to be keeping beat with the music."

"I think it's beating faster than the music." She advanced on the animated machine.

I snagged her sleeve. "You aren't going to-?"

"We need a car. Anyway, it's the risk they take."

"Well, I suppose," I hesitated, uncertain. I didn't like the idea, but at this point what did one more felony charge matter?

What's that I hear in your voice?" She gave me a speculative look. "Don't claim you never-?"

"I don't claim anything of the sort," I said with proper, red-blooded-male indignation.

Marcie took the lead toward the lively car, keeping well back from the murky windows. She leaned carefully forward and peered into the car.

I approached the left side. From the open window a female voice softly groaned. I looked inside. My impression was that of a lot of pink flesh in furious motion. The gal's eyes were squeezed shut, and the guy, well, being occupied as he was, was oblivious to everything but the task at hand.

Marcie grinned over the roof luggage rack at me, backed away, and came around the car, leaning close to my ear. "It does seem a shame to disturb them."

I shook my head. "It's a risk, remember? You want to do it, or should I?"

She winked. "I've got your back in case you get in trouble."

"That's so thoughtful of you, Miss Rose."

They'd locked the door, but the window was down enough to slide a hand inside and lift the lock. The click of the latch was conveniently masked by a sudden extreme moan of delight.

The inside light snapped on shining down upon their fully naked glory and startled faces. Their murky sensual drunkenness instantly sobered. The girl's eyes registered terror. She was a good looking; firm and ample and would probably be have to keep an eye on her weight in another few years. She instinctively curled into herself in a futile attempt at modesty.

The boy was of the tall, lanky variety, and not the least bit concerned about modesty. Anger flared in his face. "Get outta here!" he cried and lunged over the front seat at me.

I planted a palm in the middle of his chest and that sent him back on his rump.

His anger shifted fear. He'd probably heard stories about perverts who roamed the dark. The woods are full of them, if you believed the newspapers. "Hey, what's up?" His voice choked and suddenly he was fighting to hold back tears. He was only seventeen or eighteen and I felt sorry for him.

"You are, son." I grinned and glanced at his pretty girlfriend. Her blond hair was a mess but her beautiful, long eyelashes were striking. Maybe they were false. It was plain nothing else about her was. "Sorry to interrupt," I said mildly, "but we need to borrow the car."

"What are you going to do to us?" the girl said, her voice trembling, an arm folded across her breasts to hide them, a task requiring more protection than the slim limb could afford.

"We're not going to hurt you, Miss," I said, trying to sound reassuring. I didn't like the idea of what I was doing any more than she did, but any minute I expected hounds and headlights to come charging over the hill, and when that happened and the shooting began, no telling where bullets would land. "We just need the car."

"But you can't," the boy croaked, all remaining vestiges of puberty vanishing from his voice. "It belongs to my dad. He'll kill me!"

His chances of survival were better with dad than lingering here, but didn't tell him that, and reached over and unlocked the passenger door. Marcie slid inside and looked back at them. The boy's face colored and his hand moved to cover himself. Again, a limb not quite up to the task. Marcie studied him with approval and winked at the girl. "Nice hunk, honey. You've got good taste."

The girl looked dumbfounded by the remark, but I think Marcie's arrival helped tone down the fear element a little. It was cold with both doors opened.

I shut mine and switched off the radio.

"You're a music prude," Marcie said.

"I'd rather listen for dogs."

"There is that."

I said to the kids in the back seat, "You two get dressed. I'll drop you off somewhere." To Marcie I said, "Keep an eye on them."

The gear shifter felt strange, silky strange. I removed my hand and plucked off something obviously purposefully draped over it and held it to the faint light coming through the windshield. It was pink with little pink hearts embroidered all over it.

"I think she'll want those," Marcie said in a casual voice.

"Think so?" I raised an eyebrow and looked at the thin apparel in my fingers. "Probably wouldn't fit you."

She gave me a looked of someone patiently enduring an obnoxious companion. "I don't wear panties."

I laughed, "Interesting," and dangled them over my shoulder to be immediately snatched away.

I put the little car into gear, backed out of there, and crept up to the road making sure no one was coming before switching on the headlights.

Marcie found a pack of Marlboros on the dash and snatched them up. "Mind?" she asked the kids.

"They're my dad's," the boy said.

She punched in the lighter and a few moments later filled the car with smoke and gave a huge sigh.

I said, "You guys have names?"

They were silent a moment. The boy said, "I'm Jake."

"I'm Brenda," his girlfriend said quietly.

"I'm Mr. G and this is Miss R. Point me to the quickest way into town." They were scared. I couldn't blame them. I would be if the table had been turned.

They were both dressed and bundled into their coats by time I pulled into a gas station along Highway 24 and set the brake. I turned, two pairs of wide eyes staring back at me, still not convinced I wasn't some kind of serial murderer or cult leader looking for a couple young bodies to sacrifice to the God of Chaos.

"This is where you two get off. There's a phone over there. Call dad and tell him you stopped to fill the tank. Tell him you went inside to pay and Brenda went to the ladies' room, and when you came out the car was gone. It was stupid to leave the keys, but you were only gone a minute. You'll probably catch flak. I'm sorry for that, but there are some pretty bad men who will cause us all a lot of trouble if Miss R and I don't get our butts out of here quick." It wasn't my normal vocabulary, but kids nowadays understand it.

They opened their doors at the same time. "Here," I pressed a fifty into Jake's hand. He stared at it as if it had fangs. "Go on, take it. Tomorrow or the next I'll leave the car in town where it can be found. It'll have a full tank of gas. The keys will be under the mat."

I pulled away from there and onto twenty-four, heading west. "You're a pushover, Granger." Marcie blew smoke out the cracked window. "You should have just left them back there in the woods."

"You mean cold and scared, like I found you this morning?"

She winced. "All right. So you did the right thing by them."

I glanced at her and grinned.

"What?" she asked suspiciously.

"Nothing." I turned back to the dark asphalt unraveling in the headlights. According to the name on the radio face, I was driving a Datsun of some sort. What its small engine lacked in horsepower it made up for in a gutsy willingness to spin. The little mill didn't seem to mind buzzing along with the tachometer nudging seven thousand. Those revolutions per minute, held very long, would have done major damage to the little English cars I'd grown up driving.

"Nothing my—," she stopped. "Let me rephrase that. Something is plainly on your mind, Mr. Granger."

"Well actually I was thinking about what you said back there."

She blinked naively. "That I don't wear panties?" She blew smoke out the window.

I grinned over at her. "Just wondering why you would tell me something like that."

"Young Adam and Eve have given you ideas? What is it with you men?"

"It's in the hormones." I could have given a fuller biological explanation but didn't think she was really interest in hearing it.

"Well you can just forget it."

CHAPTER 7

We came out of a curve and Florissant sprang from the dark without warning. A handful of houses and few small roadside commercial buildings amounted to the sum total of this Colorado mountain village. At this time of night every window was dark and door bolted.

It's a quaint place, but I doubt it had a triple A rating on anybody's map. There's a fine little cafe off the highway, and after lunch you can drive historic Teller 1, a wide gravel road into the past...Cripple Creek.

The famous boomtown once burned with gold fever, but the heat went out of it long ago. Today, glory faded, all that remained was a collection of shacks, a main street of crumbling brick facades, and a few tourist shops. There's a pretty famous—among the locals that is—melodrama show in the basement of the old Imperial Hotel, and a lot of donkeys wandering about, but not much more. If you hike the back country, be careful where you step. Deep gold pits still pock the mountainside, some going straight down hundreds of feet. Not a place to wander about in the dark, or after having a wee bit too much to drink.

We drove through Florissant and turned off the highway onto an unmarked gravel track. You'd miss it if you didn't know the area. It wound darkly through a forest pricked with weak lights from cabins tucked into the trees. I swung onto a narrow track and bounced a few hundred feet and parked in front of a dark cabin, our headlights glaring on its door.

Marcie threw open the door and piled out, apparently seeking solid ground. Gyrating over bumpy roads more suitable to jeeps than Japanese station wagons hadn't made her happy. I'd left the key hidden under a rock and opened the place to her. She went inside while I went back to the car and killed the lights. Blackness thick enough to feel settled about the cabin. Past the tops of the tall pine trees the wide sweep of the Milky Way looked near enough to reach out and touch. The high-country stillness amplified the soft crunch of my boots on the dry pine needles as I walked to the cabin.

Marcie stood in the doorway waiting. I said, "Here we are. Home sweet home."

"Quaint and isolated. I like that."

"You wouldn't suspect it, but there're maybe fifty cabins up here within a mile of us." We went inside where the air was only marginally warmer. I'd left a small electric heater running to keep the plumbing from freezing. Marcie felt along the wall for the light switch. The blaze of a single sixty-watt bulb—at least to our dark accustomed eyes—lit the place. Marcie stopped in the middle of the small room, looked around, and headed for the refrigerator. Kitchen and living room were all one room. A bathroom was in back at the end of a hallway.

I crumpled newspaper and built a fire in the iron stove. It took a few minutes to get a proper blaze on the kindling and stack some small logs. The toilet flushed; the door swung open. "It's an ice cube in there, Granger." Marcie turned her rear to the stove. "Not much in the fridge either."

"Hadn't planned to be back here so soon if you recall. Groceries are still in the truck. Want to drive back and get them?"

"No," she said with conviction. "I'll be okay for tonight."

"You can't be hungry. Geeze, lady, you ate a twelve-dollar steak."

"I eat when I'm nervous."

"If you think it'll help there's a jar of peanut butter in one of those cabinets and some jelly in the refrigerator. Might even find some bread around here, if you don't mind a dose of penicillin with your PB&J. If not, I have frozen waffles you can toast. Go for it."

She made a face. "I'd rather stay right here and starve where it's nice and warm."

I laughed. "You're a sight warmer than you were last night." I looked her over. "Those clothes fit you like a tent."

She peered down at herself assessing the baggy garments and shrugged. "Next year the look might be all the rage on the runway."

"Considering feminine fashions these days, you might be right. I've noted recently that army boots appear to be making a comeback. The classroom keeps me on the leading edge of female fashion trends. When I started teaching, female students were skirted and coifed. Now they're trousered and booted."

"And they burn their bras, too, I hear."

"Ahem. I wouldn't know about that."

"Is that a blush I see, Mr. Granger?"

"Absolutely not."

She lost interest in the discussion and looked around the sparse cabin, her view lingering on the Royal portable typewriter a moment, and then moved to the bookcase along the wall—the only item not sparsely furnished. "You got telephone here?"

"We're not connected yet. Maybe by the end of the decade. Hopefully before the turn of the century." I grinned.

She peered at the dark windowpane. "We're pretty remote, aren't we?"

"It just appears that way."

She turned. "But there's not much chance of anyone finding us, is there?"

Whatever had scared her had burrowed itself deep in her psyche. I shrugged. "Not right off. Not tonight. If they have a good enough reason to find you and get serious about looking, they will eventually. You can't stay here too long."

"They have good reasons." She tightened her lips and thought a moment. "Where'd you say the peanut butter was?"

"Nerves?"

"Thinking about them does that to me."

"Maybe you'll feel better if you talk it out." It was

a try, but I didn't think it would get me very far.

"I'd rather console myself with a peanut butter and jelly sandwich, thank you."

"One of the cabinets. The one above the sink, I think."

She gathered the appropriate items—the bread still looked fit to eat—located a knife and went to work. "Maybe you're right, Granger. Maybe I ought to tell you," she said, busy at the counter. "You've proven trustworthy...so far." Her shoulders lifted in a small shrug. "And frankly, you're all I have at the moment."

"Thanks for the vote of confidence," I said dryly.

She peered over her shoulder. "Did I scratch thin skin?" She looked back at the sandwich she was building. "You don't write, do you?"

"Well that's out of left field. I guess it depends. Do you consider research papers writing?"

"I was referring to the popular variety. The sort normal people read."

"Normal people read research papers." I frowned, and then I knew where she was going. "Nice diversion, sweetheart. You'll not change subject so easily with me."

She grinned, carried the sandwich to a chair near the stove, and bit off a corner. "The place is finally getting warm."

I said, "Who's Cockran and what did you do to make him mad?"

She studied the sandwich in her fingers. "Cockran is head of Developmental Testing. That's his official title. More importantly Sten Cockran is buddy-buddy with Matthew Allister."

"And Matthew Allister is?"

"Founder and president of STE. He and Cockran have been friends since the war."

"Which war? We seem to be having a lot of them lately."

She narrowed toward me. "You a passivist or something? The Vietnam War, of course," she said as if there had never been any other. I reminded myself she'd only been a little girl when Vietnam ended, and suddenly I felt very old.

Marcie said, "War tends to attract strange bed fellows, you know?"

"When you're taking live fire, you don't ask the man covering your backside for a pedigree," I said.

"Maybe that's all there is to it," she agreed. "I've never met two different men than Matthew Allister and Sten Cockran. When Allister began the company, Cockran came knocking on his door looking for a job. This was all long before I started work there."

"Cockran takes his orders from Allister?"

A distant look came to her eyes. "I don't think so," she said thoughtfully. "Yes, far as the chain of command goes, he does, but somehow I have the feeling Cockran's loyalties extend beyond corporate."

"He's taking two paychecks?"

She made a face. "It's a reasonable assumption."

"Something must have clued you in. Something you read, saw, heard? A secretary might come across a variety of privy items."

She appeared to be arranging her thoughts. "At first it was just a feeling."

"Feelings are about as reliable as a politician's campaign promise."

"It's not only that. There's those three creeps he keeps around."

"Relatives? Good friends?"

She shook her head. "Anything but friends. Cockran and Alexander are always at each other."

"What does that tell you?"

She glared at me. "What does it tell you, smarty pants."

"They both get orders from someone—someone even Cockran has to answer to."

She considered that, eating the last of her sandwich. Out on the road at the end of the driveway a pair of headlights swung around the curve briefly torching the trees in front of the cabin. The car kept going, taillights bobbing around the next bend. I looked back at Marcie. "What do you have that's important enough to warrant all these sinister creeps trying to get their paws on you?"

"They think Carl told me something."

"Did he?"

"Alexander made it pretty clear they thought so. That's why they dragged me up to that cabin. It was an isolated place, and they could take their time with me."

After watching her impressive martial display earlier tonight, I had a hard time picturing anyone taking her to some isolated cabin against her will— at least not without acquiring a few broken bones along the way.

"Naturally you know nothing."

"I know nothing, Colonel Klink!" She smiled. "Sorry. I couldn't help myself. I do know some things, just not as much as they think I do." She rubbed her hands together and held them near the stove. "You don't happen to have anything to drink around here?"

"We're pretty modern ma'am. Maybe no telephone yet, but there is running water in the sink."

She rolled her eyes.

"I went to the kitchen, rummaged around one of the cabinets and came out with a dusty bottle my brother had left the last time he'd used the place. "You drink Jack Daniel's?"

"Sure. Make it a double. Neat."

There were no proper tumblers amongst the mismatched glassware, so I splashed a couple fingers of the stuff into a water glass and carried it across the room to her.

"Thanks." She took a deep pull at the glass and made a pained face. "Whew. That burns."

I was beginning to admire Marcie's stamina. When it came to alcohol, she was no lightweight. Just the same, she was hitting the stuff pretty hard tonight. Well, I wasn't in charge of her liquor intake. Maybe she had good reasons. Another time or place I might have enforced limits, but here, tonight, I figured we were safe enough. At least I didn't expect Alexander *et al* to find us so soon and burst in the door.

"You were saying?"

She glared at me over the rim of the glass. "Insistent, aren't you? Okay, for the most part they questioned me about Carl. Not directly, more like probing around the edges without coming right out and asking. Know what I mean?"

"Sure. If you really didn't know anything, they

didn't want to show their hand. Neater that way. Less explaining afterward. That is if they intended to let you go."

She winced. "I never got the impression they were going to." That thought appeared to weigh heavily on her. She drew in a breath. "So I kept evading their questions. Tried playing a little dumb, tried lying."

"Why?"

Her head snapped around. "Why?"

"If you hardly knew anything, what difference would it make if you gave honest answers to their questions?"

"You putting me on, Granger or are you naturally naive?"

I shrugged. "It comes naturally. Suppose you enlighten me?"

"I better, before you get yourself in trouble." She threw back more whiskey. "Soon as they learned all that they thought I knew; it would be over." She dragged a finger across her neck in a meaningful way. "So long as they thought I knew something of value, I was worth keeping alive. I was buying time, Granger. If Carl had told me anything, I might have told someone else. They wanted names. Why do you think I've not told you anything? The less you know the safer you are." She let go of a long sigh and peered unhappily into her whiskey glass. "Probably too late now. They'll think you were in on it from the beginning."

"Gee, that makes me feel happy."

"Thrills me too." She contemplated the glass, rolling it between her palms, and took another drink. "Carl was a thief," she said not looking up. "It's not what you think. He didn't make a career of it. A resistor or a transistor now and then, a few capacitors if whatever pet project he was concocting at home needed them. He was an electronics engineer, and like most engineers was always building something on the side."

"All bashed together with company parts."

"Mostly, I guess."

"Did STE ever miss the stolen components?"

"Inventory is never checked that closely, Granger. Besides, what's a resistor to a billion-dollar company?" Marcie looked gloomily at her drink. "A lousy resistor not worth ten cents got Carl killed."

"And one of Sten Cockran's three goons did it?"

She nodded.

"Why bounce Carl of the front bumper of a car just for pocketing a few resistors?" There was more to it that Marcie wasn't telling me. She was playing the same game, making rabbit trails like she had with those men in the cabin.

"I'm trying to figure it out. Carl came into work that morning plainly upset. He wanted to see Mr. Allister, but Allister wasn't in his office yet. Later Carl called up from the lab asking for an appointment. I told him Allister's schedule was full for the rest of the day and asked what was so urgent. He said he couldn't talk about it over the phone and mumbled something about something blowing up. On my break I went down to the assembly room to find out what was going on."

Marcie frowned at her empty glass and held it out to me to refill. "Think you ought to?"

"You're not my mother." Her words were beginning to slur again.

I dutifully refilled it. If nothing else, the liquor seemed to be oiling her tongue. When I returned, she'd lit a cigarette. "Mind?"

"I don't. My brother might."

My brother's opinion didn't matter at the moment. She puffed and drank and said, "Carl was pacing his office when I got there. I asked what was going on. He pulled out a handful of components from his pocket and held them out in his hand. Their ends were all bent and covered in solder as if he just pulled them off a PC board. They were just old, used components as far as I could see."

"Ones that he'd pilfered from STE?"

"How would I know? And he didn't have time to tell me. Sten Cockran came in at that moment, said he wanted to talk to Carl. Alone. I left him standing there, stiff as a stone, his face drained of color." She paused, drawing into herself, remembering. Her voice turned soft. "Later that morning, Carl was murdered while crossing the parking lot."

"You're sure it was murder?"

"The police said both pants pockets had been turned out. They were empty except one of the resistor component thingies that had got caught down in the lining." Marcie took another hefty drink, as if the whiskey could change anything now.

"And that's all you have to go on?"

"I have s'picion. No facts." Her shoulders rolled briefly. "I think I'm getting tipsy."

It was about time all that alcohol began showing

up, but I didn't tell her that. "Then what happened?"

"Next evening, walking out to my car, a car pulled up alongside and one of Cockran's Neanderthals yanked me through an open door and sped out of the parking lot. That was two days ago. The beginning of this nightmare." She blinked and dropped her view to the whiskey glass, watching the amber liquid rolling back and forth.

"And that's everything?" I asked. She didn't seem to hear, curled up with her thoughts as she was. She suddenly lifted a hand and pointed a finger at me, sloshing whiskey on my brother's floor in the process. "One more thing. I 'member now. One of 'em said the name Stratterford."

"Stratterford? What does it mean?"

Marcie cocked her head to one side, wearing a befuddled look that comes when you cross the line from merely drunk to totally soused. "It could mean nothing or a slot, Ganger." Her voice had fallen into a sing-songy rhythm. "What's the name of Colorado's Senator?" She tilted her head to the other side and blinked a couple times as if trying to focus.

"I don't know. I'm from New Mexico, remember?"

She leaned far forward. "Lester A. Stratterford," she said, over-pronouncing each syllable, and tipping out of the chair.

I moved to catch her, but she managed to right herself, pushing out a hand at me like a traffic cop. "I'm all right."

"You're all *wiped*. I think you've had enough," I said reaching for the glass. She pulled it away and guzzled the last of it, handing me the empty glass, flashing a crooked smile. I took it to the kitchen. When I got back, Marcie's glazed stare focused somewhere in space. I waved a hand in front of her. "Hello. Still there?"

She blinked up at me. I said, "Shall we continue?"

"What?"

"Carl mentioned something blowing up. Any idea what he meant?"

She straightened in the chair and made an effort to act sober. "I don't know, Ganger. Really don't." She shut her eyes hard and opened them. Maybe it helped to keep me in focus?

"You said STE makes detonators for nuclear war heads."

"Just the electronics."

"Could it have something to do with that?"

"I s'pose."

"Where does STE send the electronic package?"

Marcie sucked on the cigarette and flicked a long gray ash onto the pine floor. I rubbed it out with the toe of my boot. She said, "A random selection sent to Rocky Flats to be evaluated. Rest go to other manufacturers, assembled into other parts." Her words trailed off. She was making a valiant effort but losing the battle.

I took the cigarette from her fingers. "What else can you tell me?" I didn't expect much more from her tonight. "Anything about Stratterford?" Now that she'd mentioned him, I recalled reading something in the local newspaper about the Colorado Senator.

Her eyes parted and her shoulders gave a slight lift. "Don't know much 'bout him except sometimes on TV news I see him skiing or hiking. Make good campaign ads." Another lethargic shoulder lift.

I said, "How does he feel about nuclear weapons?" It was a blind shot, but it must have hit something. Her blue eyes widened; a spark of renewed vigor in them.

"He's a peacenik. One of those better red than dead crowd. That march on STE, afterwards, Senator Stratterford said he'd shut down Rocky Flats if he could. Get rid of atom bombs, he shrilled. Make a good will gesture to Soviets. Gutless bastard. A damn lot of crazy liberals voted for him. Colorado going to shithouse, Ga-Ganger. Bunch of whiny Californian hippies moving into the state. Make me sick in my stomach."

"Too much whiskey produces the same symptoms."

She glared at me. "You never said where you stood. Maybe I shouldn't be telling you this?"

"I don't discuss politics or religion, especially with young women who know judo."

"Go to hell," she said softly, her eyelids drooping and then closing. I went to the window again. The road beyond remained dark. I really didn't expect visitors, but I was keeping an eye out for headlights just the same. I turned back. Marcie's head lay to one side, her breathing slow and even. She'd put down the liquor in a serious manner tonight on top of two days in the mountains alone, on the run, cold, probably sleepless. I was surprised she lasted this long. Marcie Rose was cut from some pretty tough cloth.

Sleep is what she needed right now. I went to the bedroom, pulled back the covers, and then collected Marcie into my arms. She didn't stir. Looking down at her, she didn't look so formidable now. She was a woman with many secrets and I had the feeling some would prove to be very dark indeed, but for now she was just an exhausted young lady who'd had too much to drink and not enough sleep. She would pay for it in the morning.

I deposited her on the bed and tackled the dirty clothing, most of it still damp from tramping around in the dark. She needed pneumonia on top of all her other problems, so I just removed everything. I started to pull the covers up over her when something caught my eye. I moved the table lamp over her left breast. Beneath it and an inch to the left was a dimpled scar of pale white flesh. A second dimpled pockmark was three inches to the right of her naval. I spied a third, high up on the inside of her right thigh. I gently rolled her onto her side. A much larger and uglier scar marked her pink rump, just where I suspected it would be. Exit wounds always made a nasty mess.

There was no mistaking what had caused them. I raised a pant leg and looked at the old wound, nearly identical to the ones that marked Marcie. It had been made by nine-millimeter bullet fired from a Makarov pistol. The soldier who'd pulled the trigger discovered, to his startled last-breath dismay, that a .45 ACP fired from a nineteen-eleven was a more effective weapon. I grimaced at the memory, covered Marcie and turned the electric blanket on low.

The stove needed stoking. I fed the firebox with as many logs as it could hold, then retrieved the pistol I'd liberated from the gent back in the woods and locked it in a drawer in the small desk where my typewriter sat. The automatic's larger caliber may have offered somewhat of an advantage, but I preferred something I've shot a few thousand times. With the little Smith I was fairly certain I could hit whatever I was aiming at. I hoped I wouldn't have to aim at anything tonight.

I grabbed a box of twenty-twos off the bookshelf, filled the cylinder, and dumped a handful of the diminutive cartridges into my pocket. Before I left the cabin, I peeked in on Marcie. She'd checked out for the night and would keep until morning.

Locking the cabin's door behind me, I climbed back into the stolen station wagon.

CHAPTER 8

An all-night service station on the south end of Woodland Park provided the promised tank of gasoline. A dark Texaco station north of town provided an alleyway that faced Highway 24 more or less in the direction of the restaurant where I'd left my truck.

Rolling down the window let the cold March air into the car. With it came the occasional hum of tires from the highway. Once in a while a headlight struck up the alley, not far enough to reach me sitting in the dark car. I glanced at my watch. Ten-to-one. I played with the radio a while but couldn't find anything on this late except preachers and country and western music, so I shut it off and drummed my fingers on the steering wheel. Waiting in the dark was not something I enjoyed. At one time I'd been pretty good at it. Nowadays, a couple hours in a deer stand, or on a riverbank tempting reluctant fish are about all I'm good for.

My truck sat alone in a dim pool of light; the restaurant having been closed for a long time now.

Beyond the deserted parking lot rose the dark stand of trees from where a few hours ago Marcie and I had watched Alexander and his men stomp around in the cold. Nothing had moved down there for over an hour. If they had my truck staked out, they were professionals who knew their business. If Alexander had connections in high places, they'd have my New Mexico license plate run through the DMV in Santa Fe in the morning and find my name attached to it. It wouldn't take long after that for them to connect my name to a Thomas Granger who owned real estate in Florissant, Colorado.

Reclaiming the truck would be risky, but so would be driving around in a stolen car. Cops would be looking for it. I grimaced, switched off the car, fiddled with the overhead light so that it would stay off when the door opened, and slipped out in the cold, leaving the keys under the mat as promised. Hitching my collar to winter's sharp teeth, I strode casually down to the highway. A little way up the road an empty grocery store parking lot stood brightly illuminated to no one's benefit except maybe a local rural electric company. I steered clear of it, crossed 24, took a gravel road past the Timber Inn Restaurant and cut into the trees where Marcie and I had done damage to a couple of Alexander's thugs.

I climbed the ridge we'd found earlier and hunkered in the dark. Below, the old truck sat with one fender half illuminated. Nothing moved. No smell of cigarette smoke in the air. No errant flash of light.

I started down, stepping carefully, stopping from time to time to study the parking lot from different angles. There might have been men with rifles hidden in the shadows. A tingle shivered my spine, a familiar sensation from a long time ago. Okay, so here it was cold instead of steaming, and the vegetation needle leaf pine instead of broad leaf monsoon forests. Beyond that there really wasn't much difference. It might as well have been 1966 again. Another recon. Troops and slicks waiting just over the ridge. I tried to shake off the past but was having more trouble doing so than usual.

I moved on through the darkness, through a haze that spanned more than seventeen years. A whole lifetime to those two lovers back in the woods, I mused, suddenly feeling very old. At the edge of the trees I stopped, leaned against a dark trunk and discovered I was breathing hard, and sweating. Sweating out here in the middle of winter! I took a breath and let it slowly out. My truck was fifty yards away, the sky above clear and cold and frosted with a million tiny lights on black velvet. Familiar stars shining in familiar skies through familiar trees. The past receded and the warning-tingling that had begun earlier receded with it. With a sigh that may have been from relief or just plain exhaustion, I sat on the cold ground, leaned against the tree, took a Snickers from my pocket and quietly peeled the paper wrapper.

Marcie Rose was a liar, I decided, sitting there eating the chocolate bar and watching my truck. Marcie a liar and her dearly departed Carl a thief. It seemed reasonable that the people who wanted to get their hands on her were at least as unsavory.

What had I gotten involved in?

Well, whatever it was, I was there; I was going to have to find a way free of it all. Sitting here worrying about it wasn't going to get the job done. Fishing the keys from my pocket, I got back to my feet and walked out into the parking lot, into the light, hairs at the back of my neck bristling. No one leaped from the shadows. No bullet in the back. No sound but the crunch of my footsteps on the gravel. The door gave its squeak when I opened it and slid behind the wheel. The engine coughed reluctant awake and fell into a familiar, reassuring, rough idle.

I pulled onto the highway and took the road north toward Denver by the back way. I seemed to be pretty much alone, and that worried me a little. The rear-view mirror showed the occasional headlight that never stayed with me very long. Playing rotation? No reason to for hide and seek games unless they suspected I was good at spotting a tail, which wasn't one of the items on my curriculum vitae.

An endless forest unraveled in the truck's high beams. I'd fished a creek back here a week ago and was familiar with a topo map of the area. At West-creek, I turned off highway 67 onto an unpaved road heading more or less south. Here at least I was certain no one was following me unless they were driving with their lights off. Not likely. A bumpy half an hour later the truck crawled back onto highway 24 near the little village of Lake George. East four miles returned us to Florissant, and a couple more turns had me back at the cabin, jockeying the pickup out of sight of the road.

The stove wanted to be fed, but first I checked in on Marcie. She hadn't moved, her breathing slow and peaceful. I collected an old flannel robe, a heavy terry towel, and a bottle of shampoo from a cupboard where my brother kept such things, and placed them on the foot of the bed, and closed the door. The stove got tended to next, and then I turned out lights and curled up on the old couch that used to sit under the front room window in our parent's house.

Marcie stirred and gave a soft groan, probably wondering who'd stuffed her mouth with cotton. I set down my coffee and knocked on the door. No answer so I peeked inside. She was laying on her back, an arm over her eyes fending off the onslaught of sunlight through the east-facing window. She lifted it briefly to look at me, and groaned again, lips grinding, trying to work up some moisture.

"What time is it?" she asked, her voice about two octaves lower than a frog's croak.

"Nearly ten."

"In the morning?"

"Generally speaking, at this latitude the sun doesn't shine at ten o'clock in the night."

"Ha, ha."

"Coffee's brewed and breakfast can be ready in fifteen minutes if you think you're up to eating anything.

"What happened last night?" Her tone carried a larger question than just those simple words. I grinned.

"Nothing of any great importance. You did a lot of drinking and talking, and then passed out."

She lifted her arm again, staring. "You sure?"

"Fairly." I knew where she was heading.

She covered her eyes again and smacked her lips a couple times. "I might not be totally with it this morning, Granger, but I'm aware enough to know I'm completely naked under this blanket. Is there something I ought to know about?"

I laughed. "I prefer my ladies scrubbed and combed, and responsive. You're naked because I removed your damp and dirty clothes and tucked you under a nice, warm electric blanket so you wouldn't come down with pneumonia. Don't worry, your virtue is intact . . . oh, and by the way, you must have been mistaken when you said you didn't wear panties."

She smiled briefly. It's seemed to pain her parched lips. "You had to find out for sure, didn't you?"

"Think of it as research. There's shampoo and a towel and the cabin has hot running water."

She glanced at the pile on the bed. "Such luxuries. Real twentieth century convinces way out here."

I closed the door and puttered in the little kitchen getting breakfast together. The bedroom door opened a few minutes later, the bathroom door closed, and soon the shower was running.

I had the table set—pancakes, maple syrup—the real stuff—butter and bacon—when Marcie emerged from the bathroom wrapped about in my brother's robe. She made her way over carefully and sat quietly, taking a sip of water that waited for her there. She gently set the glass back on the table.

"Coffee?"

Her head barely nodded. Probably all she could manage without it hurting too much. "That awful whiskey of yours," she said.

"I recall you claiming something about being a big girl."

Marcie made a face. "Hope I didn't make a fool of myself. No striptease in the middle of the living room floor?"

"Nothing so entertaining, unfortunately." She either really didn't remember or she was testing me? I decided to find out. "You did tell me who you really worked for." Okay, so I was a liar too.

She stared at the pancakes a moment, then smeared butter on them. "Did I?"

"You did." That was about all I dare say without tipping my hand.

She drew in breath and let it out, her eyes curiously fixed upon me, her voice cautious. "So I let the cat slip the bag."

I took a bite of pancake to keep from having to answer.

"Hmm. So, what's your opinion of female reporters who go undercover to get a story?"

"I have no opinion," I said figuring that was a safe answer.

A quick smile flashed to her lips. Just as quickly her expression went flat. "Did I tell you why I wormed my way into a job at STE?"

I crawled out on a very shaky limb. "Something about investigative reporting."

"Investigative reporting? Did I really call it that in my drunkenness? You got a cigarette? No, of course you don't." She looked about. "Where'd I put that pack?"

I retrieved the crumpled pack from the bookshelf. She fumbled a cigarette from it and took a light from a stick match. Tom had left a box of them to light the propane stove.

She puffed her cigarette and seemed to relax. "Actually, it was an exposé." Her voice was no longer hesitant but confident. "The Gazette got wind of a story and pulled some strings. Next I knew, I was being hustled into STE to ferret out the truth of it. Did I tell you that?"

I didn't like the direction this was taking, and I didn't like having to lie to get at what she'd been hiding. It felt too much like I was playing Marcie's game, and in some odd way, Carl's too. I shrugged. "You weren't very lucid toward the end."

She lingered a while with the coffee, and then moved a piece of pancake about in a smear of syrup. Maybe she was debating how far to go with this story. Or maybe like me, she was making it up as she went along. "Sten Cockran has a checkered past. Hardly the sort of person who could pass a background check for the security clearance he had at STE. Did I mention that?"

"You did."

"I have a big mouth when I drink. What else did I—" she stopped abruptly, her head snapping around at the knock at the door; a light, rapid tap that I recognized instantly and brought on a sudden wave of panic.

"It's all right," I said quietly motioning to the bedroom. "Make yourself scarce."

"Who—" she mouthed.

"Later," I whispered, and gathered up the dishes and deposited them in the sink. "Be right there," I called, took a calming breath, waited for the bedroom door to latch. I stuck a hand casually in my pocket and went to the door.

"Paul, darling." Bundled in her furs and kid leather, brown eyes smiling warmly, Sherri flashed an orthodontic-perfect smile. She wore her usual lipstick, *Morning Frost*. I didn't particularly care for the color. When I'd mentioned it once, she told me it had been recommended by some fashion stylist, and that settled the matter. It made her lips look cold, but when she stretched to kiss me, those cold lips burned with passion.

It was a short kiss and she hurried past me. "Close that door, darling, you're letting in all the cold." She drew off her gloves and pushed pink fingernails through her shiny brown hair, "I didn't really expect to find you back so soon, but it was Saturday, and that dreadful meeting at the Club was postponed until April, so I decided to drive up and take a chance."

Sherri unbuttoned her coat. "I almost drove right past without stopping when I didn't see that old truck parked out front. Luckily, I saw it in the mirror at the top of the hill. You parked it behind the cabin. Why did you do that?" Before I could answer she changed subjects. "I think the stove needs wood, darling, it's frightful in here. Well, aren't you happy to see me? Why are you so closed-mouth?" Sherri threw her arms around my neck and kissed me again. She stopped, sniffed the air and said, "Coffee smells delicious." She headed for the kitchen.

"You don't want to go in there. The sink's a mess," I said taking her hand and turning her toward the couch.

"That never bothered you before."

I grinned, "Maybe I'm beginning to feel self-conscious about my sloppy bachelor ways. I'll get coffee. Make yourself comfy on the couch. I'm going to have to be leaving here shortly anyway."

"Leaving?" *Morning Frosted* lips pouted.

"I have to see a fellow down in the Springs at the university about some research material." I was lying again, and I didn't like it. It was for her safety, I told myself, and that was partly true. Whatever I'd gotten myself entangled with; I didn't want Sherri to be a part of it.

"You're supposed to be on vacation, darling."

I laughed. "It's called a sabbatical and I'm *supposed* to be working. That's why the university gives them. They expect a publication out of me in some prestigious scientific journal, with their name prominently mentioned, of course."

"Wish I'd known," Sherri said dramatically. "Does that mean we can't be together today?"

"I'm disappointed too." I carried a cup of coffee to her.

"I had Klaus take the top off this morning. I was hoping it would be warm enough this afternoon for a brisk drive in the mountains. With you sitting beside me."

"I wasn't supposed to be home, remember? Fortunately, I remembered the appointment when I did and cut the fishing short." I grinned at her pout. "Anyway, a drive with the top down will mess your hair."

"Well there is that." Sherri played with the pearls about her neck. "If not today, then when?"

"I'll be tied up getting all the data together at least until Wednesday. You know how I've been putting off compiling those population density graphs."

"Wednesday is half a week away. You should buy yourself one of those little Apple thingys. You'd have your old graphs done at a push of a button, and then we could spend time together."

"I can't justify buying a microcomputer when the university has a real IBM I can use."

"Daddy would buy it for you," she said.

To Sherri, daddy's checkbook could fix everything. "They're toys, Sherri. Another fad like hula-hoops and pet rocks. They'll never be useful for anything but playing Space Invaders."

"You're being stubborn, Paul. You know you ought to listen to me more. With my help we could make something—." She stopped and looked embarrassed. "What I meant to say was—"

"What you meant to say is, with you and your father's connections, this lowly biology teacher might actually amount to something someday." I said it gently, but she'd touched a nerve, and it hadn't been the first time.

Sherri's eyes got large and sincere. "Oh, Paul darling, that isn't what I meant at all." An elfish smile picked at the corners of her mouth when she saw that I wasn't really angry with her. "You're teasing. You're such a beast, Paul. Why do you enjoy hurting me?"

"Because you're a champ. You never stay down for the count."

She wrapped her arms around my neck again and brought her face close to mine. Her big, brown eyes were inviting, the faint odor of perfume lingering about her hair. "What I meant to say is we could make something of *our* lives...together, darling." Her orthodontic perfect smile sparkled, matching the fiery sparkle of her diamond earrings set ablaze by the morning sunlight through the front window. "Why do I love you so much, darling?" she whispered gazing into my eyes. "You really are a beast. Why do I put up with you?"

I wrapped my arms around her and pulled her close. "Oh Paul," she said breathlessly when we finally broke from the kiss. "When I'm with you like this I never want to leave. Do you have to go into town today?" Brown eyes widened hopefully. "I can think of a more pleasant way to spend the day. We can build a fire and throw a blanket on the floor. I have a bottle of Champagne out in the car."

I gently separated us. "You build a tempting picture," I told her truthfully, my thoughts distracted by the other woman I'd stashed away in the bedroom. Marcie was probably listening at the keyhole. I grimaced. Suddenly I had more females on hand than I knew what to do with. I'm not opposed to a rush of pretty, young women so long as they don't come at me so quickly that they begin to pile up. "But not today."

She fitted a pout to her iced lips. "I don't understand how picking apart baby rock flies and staring at them under a microscope could be more important than me...us being together."

"Stone flies."

"Stone flies, then. I just don't understand."

"It's my work, Sherri. It's what I do." I'd told her that more than once but it didn't seem to matter to her.

"Yes, I know. It's your work." The pout eased a little. "Well, if I do have to turn right around and drive thirty-five miles back down the mountain, I'm at least going to take that cup of coffee you promised."

"I'll get it," I said turning her to the couch. She sat and opened her purse on the floor rummaging through it for a mirror and a golden cylinder of lipstick to repair the minor damages we'd inflicted on the makeup. I went to the kitchen, found a couple clean cups and filled them.

Sherri said from the living room, "Maybe we can meet for dinner this evening, Paul?" I heard her footsteps. "I can make reservations at Charles Court...my treat. I know the maitre de. I can get an excellent ta-" her words broke off "-ble." The last syllable finished itself as if forced from her lips; her wide eyes staring at the kitchen table and the two plates and two cups of coffee there. Sherri was not a dumb brunette despite her sometimes-Pollyannaish view of healing the world. I watched the warmth in her eyes turning cold and her back stiffening. She stood there in the kitchen doorway a long moment and then slowly turned her head toward the closed bedroom door.

"You have someone in there, don't you, Paul."

I nodded.

"You really didn't intend to go into town today."

"It's not what you think, not as in appears," I said lamely, two cups of coffee in my hands.

"I think I want to leave now." Her voice was icy.

I followed Sherri into the living room, set the coffees on an end table. "Sherri, let me explain."

She buttoned her coat and pulled on gloves. "I don't want to hear your explanation. I don't want to talk to you right now. I've already made a perfect fool of myself."

I stepped in front of the door. She looked up sharply, her eyes shining. "Let me leave."

"Sherri, it isn't what you think."

"I wasn't born yesterday, Paul," she snapped and pushed past me, tugging the door open. I followed her outside into a bright, morning sun and watched her go down the path to the driveway. She slipped into the cream-colored Mercedes and slammed the door. The steel roof had been removed and the fabric top fitted in place. The engine purred to life and the rear tires kicked up a cloud of dust and stones as she sped away. Behind me, padded footsteps approached.

"That was awkward."

I turned. Marcie was smaller than Sherri, not nearly as tall or as broad in the shoulders, but there was nothing frail or fragile about the woman who looked up into my face. Except for gender, Marcie and Sherri were really nothing at all alike. Where Sherri could never be comfortable in anything but the finest dresses or jeans with expensive names embroidered across the back pocket, Marcie appeared at ease in her baggy, borrowed pants and shirt. Where Sherri had the ability to express honest, simple warmth, Marcie seemed always on guard, always wary. Where Sherri's soft, smiling face had difficulty expressing any degree of anger beyond that which might be appropriate toward a maitre de who'd had the temerity to seat her at a wrong table, Marcie seemed to wear a perpetual hard and hungry look. Maybe I was making too much of the comparison. I remembered the pancakes still on our plates on the table. Hell, maybe Marcie wore that hungry look because she really was hungry?

"You really care for her, don't you? I'm sorry I screwed things up for you, Granger. She'll be back."

Maybe I really did care for Sherri more than I'd realized until just now. At the moment I was confused, and yes, hurt, although I hid that feeling behind tough exterior. I said, "Our breakfast is getting cold. We better eat it before it turns to ice too."

CHAPTER 9

By the time we got back to our breakfast it was cold. I didn't feel much like eating now anyway. Marcie's appetite seemed to have left her too. I suspected that was more a reaction to my own suddenly somber mood than to the cold plate of food in front of her.

"She'll come back," Marcie said, interrupting my thoughts. She pushed away her plate of untouched pancakes. "She's just like me. A sucker for the tall, handsome, silent type."

I knew what she was trying to do, and I appreciated the effort. I wanted to tell her that Sherri and she were nothing at all alike, but I'd already worked through that idea. I said, "At least the coffee is still hot. I can stick those in the oven for you."

"I wasn't talking about coffee, Paul."

"I know." The morning had turned sour and suddenly I wanted to be somewhere else—anywhere but my brother's cramped little cabin in the pines. "Come on," I said standing.

"Where are we going?"

"Down to the Springs. I know of a little golf club restaurant there where the cooking is light years ahead of mine."

"Should we? I mean..."

I grinned. "Colorado Springs is a big, grown-up town nowadays. Our chances of getting in and out of it without being noticed are pretty good, don't you think?"

"Well...I suppose." She paused. "You planning on seeing someone?"

I looked at her sharply.

She averted her gaze. "Sorry. I just thought that maybe you were going to chase after her, that's all."

"Sherri will keep for now. My personal problem can wait until we take care of yours." I put away everything that would spoil if left out then shrugged into my coat and checked the revolver still in the pocket. I locked the place up and we went around back to where the truck was parked.

Marcie slid into the seat beside me. "The highway may be watched."

"Maybe," I said. "I'm half counting on it."

She looked at me oddly, questioningly.

I said, "Them finding us will save us the time and trouble of us finding them. I'd as soon get this over with quickly. I don't much care for looking over my shoulder all the time."

"That's reckless talk, Granger." She was scowling.

I gave a wry smile, shoved the gear shifter into reverse, and backed out onto the gravel road. "In that case, it ought to be right up your alley."

She huffed. "Not hardly, macho man."

"You disapprove?" We came to the highway and turned left toward Colorado Springs.

"I know them. The games they play are no fun."

Ten minutes later I picked up a tail. He'd been waiting for us in a Safeway parking lot in Woodland Park. I didn't tell Marcie as I watched him in my rear-view mirror. We left the little town and funneled out onto a divided highway and started down Ute Pass. Dropping in elevation, the topography and vegetation changed; low shrubs and scrub oak replacing tall pines. We swept past Manitou Springs and leveled off into Colorado Springs sprawling up the Eastern slope of the Rocky Mountains. I always thought eastern Colorado unlovely compared to the mountain scenery. It reminded me a little of Portales; flat, monotonous, tawny land stretching away in all direction except west, of course. There the timbered real estate soared ruggedly to the fourteen-thousand-foot pinnacle of naked-rock known as Pikes Peak.

Marcie looked nervous, studying me through narrowed eyes. "What's wrong?"

Had I been that transparent? "Nothing," I said, which wasn't totally a lie. The gent behind us hadn't made his move yet.

"You don't sound disappointed?"

I smirked. "Despite what you may think, Marcie, I'm not."

"Back there you made it sound like you were going fishing and we were the worm."

"We are, but if I have to do any fancy driving, this old pickup might end up on its top. I'd rather choose the time and place to reel them in." I watched the road ahead and took the appropriate turn off the highway heading north. Maybe I was just naive enough to believe that if we kept a low profile long enough it might all blow over. Maybe that red Porsche behind us belonged to a gent who just happened to be going the same direction we were. And maybe that was all wishful thinking. "On the other hand," I continued, "I don't intend to keep my head under the covers very long, and if that means having it out with them, then bring it on. I've gone up against worse in Nam, and from what little I've learned about you, Miss Rose, I suspect you have too."

She looked at me long and probing. "That's the most you've said since leaving the cabin. Don't over think who or what I am."

"Touchy this morning, aren't we?"

She turned away staring out the windshield.

I downshifted and took a right onto Garden of the Gods Road.

"Why are we going this way?" She asked in a wary voice.

"It's how we get to that restaurant I told you about." Her stare narrowed suspiciously. I grinned. "And I'm curious to see the place where you work."

"Thought so. It's probably being watched."

"Maybe, but I suspect it's one of the last places they'd expect you to show up."

"Hope you're right, Granger. I don't particularly want to be here, and I think you're not taking any of this seriously enough, or are you trying to show me what a tough hombre you are?" The strain in her voice sounded genuine.

"Now who's over thinking? If it makes you feel better, I hope I'm right too."

She drew in a short breath, and frowning she pointed. "It's up that road ahead."

I cranked the wheel over and turned onto a wide, newly paved road that appeared to have been cut though a rancher's cow pasture. I'd read somewhere that all this land had been owned by the Flying W Ranch at one time. They sold off a lot of it to the developers but kept a small cow/calf outfit to the west, and their famous Flying W Chuckwagon attraction that drew a considerable number of tourists and locals during the summer season.

For the last seven or eight years, this part of Colorado Springs has been developing into something of a Silicon Valley east—the locals referred to it as Silicon Mountain. Computer and scientific entrepreneurs were popping up all over the place, gobbling up land once occupied by fat and contented cows.

The paved road ended abruptly in a field of yucca. Where you find yucca, you can bet the natural ecology of the area had been disturbed. Yucca is a successional species that takes over when the natural equilibrium of the biome has been disrupted by something—hungry cows in this case. It's actually a member of the lily family, not a cactus as many folks tend to refer to it. And that's the biology lesson for today. Class dismissed.

"There," Marcie said pointing, pulling my attention from the local flora. I set the brake and studied the low, modern, concrete building, more warehouse-looking than high tech, vaguely styled in the southwestern fashion. I grew up in New Mexico and it didn't look anything at all southwesternish except for its ado-be-brown paint and softened corners. The building sprawled here and there like a housing development on steroids. A huge parking lot consumed a sizable chunk of land. A small rectangle in front of the build-ing was grassed and landscaped with non-indigenous vegetation guaranteed to die the first time the grounds keeper forgot to turn on the sprinkler system—well, it's all automatic these days, but the end results would be the same. Without constant watering and care it was bound to whither, die, and surrender the land back to the nearly indestructible yucca.

Marcie said, "Okay, you've seen it. Let's get out of here."

I killed the engine, leaned across the wide steering wheel, and looked the neighborhood over. A field of yuccas separated Space Technologies and Electronics from its neighbor. The building was two stories and clad in acres of black glass. Its parking lot covered a con-siderable amount of real estate too, and like STE's, was practically devoid of cars on this Saturday morning.

"What's that?" I asked, pointing.

"Hewlett-Packard." She turned her blue eyes toward me. "Just what are you looking for anyway?"

If it had been a buck and I a hunter with a tele-scopic sight on my rifle, I'd have judged the distance from my truck to that parking lot to be somewhere around three hundred and fifty yards. A rather long shot but not overly so for one of the more robust, flat-shooting calibers available these days. Not too long a shot for an accomplished marksman, which few men who take to the mountains today in deer season are. But I wasn't a hunter today, and it wasn't a buck that interested me. The driver of the bright red Porsche must have thought three hundred and fifty yards was a safe enough distance to wait us out.

I looked away from the car. If he had a pair of field glasses trained on us, I didn't want him to think I was the least bit interested in his arrival. I thought it a joke, anyway. Who'd use an expensive sports car several shades brighter than a fire engine to tail a man and woman in an antiquated pick-up truck just barely capable of breaking the national, Stasi enforced double-nickel speed limit.

It was all wrong. I'm no authority on tailing people but it did seem reasonable to me that a person intent on engaging in such activities would choose something less conspicuous. A '72 Ford Fairlane or Chevy Belair maybe, not the fat tire, low stance, aggressively hungry look of a Porsche Carrera—well, I couldn't be sure of the model, but it was flashy as hell and one heck of a hard vehicle to not notice.

Marcie cleared her throat. "I seem to recall something said about breakfast?"

"The little tummy complaining?"

"At times you can be a very annoying man."

I started the truck and backed it around. Marcie said, "I get the feeling like I'm drifting through a fog. You've got something cooking up there," She pointed at my head, "that you're not telling me. What is going on?"

"Suppose you tell me." The gearbox clunked into second. First is the granny gear and strictly for climbing rocks or pulling tree stumps.

"I've already told you-"

"You've told me nothing, sweetheart, except carefully fabricated stories to throw me off whatever trail you're trying to hide."

Marcie straightened around on the seat and stared through the windshield. "All right, what is it you want me to tell you?"

"You can begin with who you called on the telephone last night from the restaurant. Her head snapped around and her mouth parted slightly in surprise. "From there we can progress to more interesting subjects like who you really work for."

I shifted up to third and drove past the parking lot where the Porsche sat. An open newspaper hid the man's face. As I suspected, a pair of field glasses were on the dash.

CHAPTER 10

Marcie returned her gaze out the front window as we pulled back onto Garden of the Gods. In profile she had attractive, high cheek bones that suggested a strain of Native American ancestry—well, Native American is the term everyone seems to be using these days. I've always considered it somewhat sloppy nomenclature. I was born in Santa Fe, New Mexico, so technically speaking that makes me as Native American as any Navaho or Apache, in spite of a curious predilection among some easterners to inquire if the monetary exchange rate in New Mexico is the same as that of the United States. The terms aboriginal or Amerindian seem more precise, although those have fallen out of fashion.

The morning sunlight made her brown hair shine. It was definitely brown and not black, which I thought would have gone well with the arch of her cheeks. Maybe it had been black at one time? That sort of thing is hard to tell these days. Don't get me wrong, I like all the natural colors, it's the tie-dye hairdos beginning to show up in the classrooms that I have a problem with.

I had the truck rolling in third gear. In the rear-view the Porsche was just turning out of the parking lot in no great hurry. He could afford to take it easy. No way was this old Ford going to outrun him.

"I'm waiting," I prodded.

She exhaled sharply. "What I told you was the truth. I am a reporter. I'm working undercover. That's all there is, and I don't know why you're making a Federal case out of it."

"Do newspapers really insert reporters into large organizations with false identifies? I'll be first to admit that I know next to nothing about the newspaper business, but it sounds to me like an invite for a big lawsuit."

Her lips tightened in exasperation. "Why do you think I hesitated telling you anything about myself? When I asked you if you did any writing did it even occur to you that I was trying to protect my story? No, suspicious you only thought I was stalling, hiding some deep secret." She shot a hot glare my direction. "I wasn't about to pass along a tip if I thought there was the slightest chance you might run with it and scoop me. A reporter's story is damn near the most sacred thing a reporter has and even you should realize that."

It was a good story. I was almost convinced, but not quite. There was more she wasn't telling. I'd heard one yarn after another, and none of them had been true. "You're really very good but you'll have to do better than hurtful looks and a tale about protecting your precious story. And you've managed to nicely tap-dance around my first question."

She began to say something in protest then stopped herself, the anger melting into a smirk. "I'm on to you, Granger. You're playing the consummate fisherman now, aren't you? Playing out the line nice and easy, just enough at a time to keep me talking. Don't want to reel her in too quickly now, do we? Give the lady a little more slack, let her fight the hook, wear herself out while you enjoy the sport of it. Is that the game you're playing? You were pretty good just now. You got something I didn't want to give. Well, Mr. Angler this fish is heading for deep water where all the snags hang out."

I laughed. "That was pretty good. Maybe you really are a writer." I glanced at the man in the mirror four cars behind us. "Whether or not you care to admit it, we've got real trouble with real men who carry real guns. They—whomever they are—are closing in on you and me and unless you start telling me what's going on, you and me, we're going down, as they say in the movies. And don't give me that woeful look and say you don't know what I'm talking about. You're no reporter, at least not for any legitimate newspaper. You fight like Bruce Lee, you handle a gun like Roy Rogers, and you carry enough bullet wounds on your lily-white body to qualify for a handful of Purple Hearts and probably a Congressional Medal of Honor depending on what side of the fence you got them on."

We were coming to a stoplight. I swung into a fast food parking lot near the corner and pulled into a space facing the street. The Porsche stopped at the light, the plaid-capped gent behind the wheel keeping his eyes straight ahead, the binoculars no longer on the dash. Probably on the seat beside him.

"Before you say anything, take a good look at the driver in that red car."

She did. I said, "Do you recognize either the car or the driver?" The light changed and he moved off with the traffic.

"I don't," she said looking at me. "Should I?"

I said, "I don't know. We picked him up in Woodland Park just before the highway divided. He's been tailing us ever since. He waited in the lot down below STE with a pair of binoculars, 10x50 judging from what I was able to see of them. He's got a two-way radio, probably a FM if I'm reading that short second antenna on the left fender correctly."

I could tell that had shaken her, but Marcie's voice remained remarkably calm and professional. "They've found us." I had the impression tight fixes and sudden changes in plans were not an uncommon thing for her."

"It would appear so, but they don't seem to be in any hurry to do anything about it. Any ideas why?" I'm certain she had a few, but I didn't expect getting the information out of her was going to be so easy. It wasn't.

"No. And wipe that suspicious look off your face. I'm telling you the truth. I have no idea who that man is or why he's playing cat and mouse with us." Her view darted back to the spot by the light but the Porsche had already moved off. She looked at me a little uncertainly. "You sure about all this or are your nerves getting the better of you?"

Marcie was right, of course. Given the right combination of nervous stimulus and imagination a person could take a string of coincidences and build a pretty good case out of them, but not this time. I grimaced. It had been a lot of years since I'd played a game like this. Back then I'd been a pawn on an international chess board. Today, well I didn't know what it was all about, but once you spend a few youthful years weaving and dodging the other pawn's moves, it sort of becomes like riding a bike. No, I hadn't forgotten what it felt like to know I was being followed. I might have been a little unsteady in the beginning, but I was getting my balance back. And I hadn't forgotten that queer itch between my shoulder blades that won't go away when scratched.

I said, "What do you want to bet that there'll be a very expensive tail in my mirror if they haven't changed cars. They should. I don't understand why they haven't already. I get the feeling this is all pretty new to them."

"But not to you?" She looked at me accusingly. "You seem to know a lot about being followed."

I said, "I played this game once before—well, several times before. It was a different part of the world, but the same game. The game never changes, only players and location." I got the truck moving again trying not to remember like I do sometimes at night, when dreams turn ugly. "I didn't like it back then and I don't like it now. It's not my past I'm interested in. It's yours, Miss Rose. Not the whole thing, of course, just the parts that relate to why you and I are here and why we are of enough interest to anyone to latch a tail onto us." I glanced over. She was staring straight ahead. I continued, "That was pretty fancy, the way you took out that gent last night. Taekwondo? Is that what they're teaching in journalism school these days?"

"Taekkyeon. My parents lived and worked in South Korea for the first twelve years of my life. I was interested in martial arts. They paid for the lessons, but we moved back to the States before I was very competent. I got the rest of my training at the taxpayer's expense in the army."

There was a certain triumph in her voice that I was learning was characteristic of Marcie whenever she felt she'd pulled a trump card on me. I shifted into third and rolled through the green light at Nevada Avenue, bouncing across the highway while traffic piled up on the north and south bound lanes. We were going east and I realized that the Garden of the Gods Road had vanished and this was a new street. Well, it hadn't really gone away. It was the same strip of concrete, only the name changed when we'd crossed Nevada. The street sign informed me we were now on Austin Bluffs Parkway, thank you very much. I'd come this way before, but this was the first time I'd noticed the name change. It's an easy thing to overlook when you're not paying attention, when all your senses aren't tuned finer than an Indy 500 race car.

It was not so easy, however, to overlook the red Porsche that pulled slowly into view and settled two cars behind us in the same comfortable spot where it had been since leaving Woodland Park. I grimaced at a thought. Maybe he didn't want to go unnoticed?

Maybe keeping my attention on what was behind us instead of what was ahead had been his plan all along?

Marcie was saying, "While in the employ of our esteemed uncle with the white beard, I lucked into an assignment with the Stars and Stripes. It's a-"

"I know what the Stars and Strips is," I said cutting short her glib patter. "You're doing a lot of talking but you aren't saying much."

"After I was discharged," she went on, a touch of annoyance in her voice, "I went to work for a little newspaper in Virginia called the *Old Dominion.*"

I glanced at her.

"Honest, that was its name. Virginia is close to DC, don't you know?"

I rolled my eyes. She smirked and continued, "I quite often covered the political scene, but unfortunately, the *Dominion* was a small rag with an even smaller budget, and that meant low-rent lodging in the seedier parts of the District for staff on assignments. If you've ever been to DC, you know what I'm talking about. Most of the time I was alone. I felt particularly vulnerable every time I stepped out of the cab and walked those long, dark steps up to my motel room. I fell back on my army training, and on the side earned a black belt in Aikido."

"I thought you said it was Taekkyeon?"

She laughed. "Try to find someone in the States who teaches Taekkyeon, let alone is a master in the art."

It made sense, so I let the discrepancy ride.

"I still take lessons on and off when I feel I need to brush up. I don't fight competition anymore. I know my capabilities and I don't enjoy being knocked around by someone who can do it better than me."

We were passing the university—UCCS to the locals—and I cranked the steering wheel hard and beat a yellow light into the university parking lot. The Porsche hit the red and stopped. I drove slowly toward the little machine at the curb. I didn't want to lose him now. The machine demanded an offering of quarters in exchange for a parking stub. I didn't have any quarters to sacrifice and I drove on through into the sparsely populated lot and pulled into a slot under some trees at the far end.

Marcie had suspended her story when I'd nearly put the truck on its side making the turn. She glanced around at the brown lawn and leafless trees scattered amongst the green firs and said, "What are you up to, Granger?" She looked over her shoulder out the rear window.

"Our friend in the Porsche is persistent. It's time we find out who he is and what he wants." That brought a smile to Marcie's face. "Figured that might satisfy your blood lust for a while."

She said, "He's taken the bait."

'Don't appear too interested. I see him in the outside mirror. He's feeding the money-gulping machine. Got a ticket."

"At least he's legal," Marcie said.

"And we know he travels with a pocketful of change."

Marcie frowned. "Somehow I didn't picture him as the legal sort."

I shrugged. "Never can tell how some folks arrange their morals. Here he comes. He's driving around to the far end of the lot, pulling under that stand of old blue spruce." The trees looked old enough to have been some of the original plantings way back before this had been a university, back when all this had been a tuberculosis sanitarium in the thirties. "We'll give him a few minutes to wonder what we're up to. In the meantime, I'd like to hear about the time Roy Rogers gave you shooting lessons?"

She scowled. "You just don't give up, do you?"

"And you're about one lie away from being booted out of here so that I can go back to the mountains and find a nice, quiet fishing hole to drown worms in until whatever it is that's brewing here blows over, so better make it good."

"I see no reason why I have to explain my life to you."

I nodded. "You're right. No reason at all. There's the handle. Give it a good tug and the door opens."

Her lips came together practically turning blue. Lockjaw, I decided, was a reoccurring condition with Marcie, sort of like malarial fevers.

"I was born on a ranch in northern Arizona, about thirty miles from Mesa," she blurted all at once, inhaled sharply and glared at me. "I had three brothers who could and could shoot like...like Roy Rogers, all right? They looked after grandpa's cattle and I had two choices. Either learn to ride and shoot well enough to keep up with them or stay home with my mother and little sister and learn to sew and cook and put up vegetables. I opted for riding and shooting."

"Was that before or after you lived in South Korea?" I inquired giving her a skeptical look. She had so many stories they were beginning to trip over each other."

"Anyone ever tell you how annoying you can be?"

"I think you may have—once or twice."

Her lips got tight again, and she stared out the windshield at the old, white, sanitarium building framed in naked tree branches. It was an attractive piece of early Colorado Springs architecture with pink tiled triangular projections on the roof like miniature great pyramids. The building once housed the main tubercular hospital way back when this architectural style had been in vogue. Today it looked sadly out of place among the newer, less inspired classrooms sprouting like weeds across the campus, all angles and no imagination, no beauty.

She looked back at me and there was a sheen in her eyes. "Both, if you must know. I was born in Arizona, and then moved with my parents to Seoul when I was two. My father was a civil engineer and had been hired to oversee a railroad being built through some pretty rough countryside. He was away a lot." She grimaced. "Alicia was born in Korea. That was a hard pregnancy for Mom. She never could get use to the heat and humidity, and the culture, so we moved back to Arizona. My brothers were all older than me and were a big help around the ranch. Grandpa Saavadra was in his eighties and couldn't work like he used to."

Marcie went quiet for a moment with her memories. "What I remember best were the warm summer evenings camping out under the stars—there were so many were we lived, away from city lights. I would curl up on my sleeping bag reading a Victoria Holt novel in the light of a Coleman lantern while my brothers sat around the campfire quietly telling dirty jokes and lying about the horses they'd ridden and the girls they'd loved." A smile lingered on Marcie's lips, slowly sagging into a frown. "Grandpa lost the ranch to the land bank over a loan he'd taken out a decade before. The place had been part of a Spanish land grant and had been in our family for over two hundred years. Mom grew up there and Dad had come to love it as if he had too. We had to move into the city. I think the heartbreak of that is what killed Grandpa the next year. A couple years after that Mom got cancer. Curt got drunk and drove his pickup into an irrigation ditch and life just sort of went to hell.

"I was twenty-one. Dad took a job with the Santa Fe Railway, and just like in Korea, he was gone a lot. Mom died on Christmas Eve while Dad was somewhere between Chicago and La Junta. With Mom gone there was nothing left for me—for any of us—in Mesa. Alicia was eighteen and away at college. Rodney had gone to work for a local grain and feed distributor. Mark got married and now sells hardware at a *Handy Dan* in California. And me-?, I joined the army."

I said, "Is that where you got shot up?"

Marcie shook her head, and then grinned at me. "It wasn't those bullet wounds you were looking at, Granger. You can't tell me that."

"I'd be a liar if I said I didn't notice the rest of the assets."

"Like what you saw?"

I shrugged. "You're sort on the skinny side, but then I like women on the skinny side. You might have stirred up a certain amount of lust within my wicked soul."

"Regretting not taking me up on my offer last night?"

If she was playing a game to distract me from my suspicious questions, she was doing a pretty good job of it. "There'll be other opportunities," I said with proper male hubris.

Her eyebrows arched. "Think so?"

I grinned. "One can hope." In the outside mirror I glimpsed a flash of light from inside the Porsche.

Marcie said, "The wounds are more recent than my army days. I was covering a story in Nicaragua two summers ago. The bus I was riding on was stopped by Sandinistas. The driver got out and was having what appeared to be a cordial conversation with one of the men I assumed was the leader. For some reason that I've never been able to determine, they opened fire on the bus with machine pistols. I was one of the lucky ones. I awoke in a hospital in Puerto Cabezas, on the Caribbean coast." She grimaced. "Like I said, I was lucky. Several of my compadres were not." Marcie paused seeing my attention suddenly fixed on the door mirror. "What is it?"

"He's getting curious. Just put those binoculars on us." I looked away from the mirror. "All right, I believe you...halfway. I still have questions, but they'll have to wait. I suppose you know how to drive a pickup truck?"

"Granger, you weren't listening. I was practically born in a pickup truck, and there's more truth to that than just a tired old cliché."

"Just testing you." I grinned. "Don't get your pretty, skinny self in a tizzy. I'm going to go into the administration building, that place with the pyramids on its roof. It doubles as classrooms too. I want you to slide over here behind the wheel and keep an eye on the mirror but try not to act interested. Pretend you're bored, or napping. When I give you the signal, drive over and pull behind the Porsche in case he decides to try something tricky. Got it?"

"Aye, aye, captain." She gave a mock salute.

I opened the squeaky door and left her sitting there. Maybe putting her in charge of the truck was my way of showing her I really did believe the story she'd told, or maybe I was trying to convince myself it was all true. Whatever the deep psychological reasons were, it was a mistake. I should have said to hell with Marcie Rose's feelings and driven away from there just as far and as fast as the old truck would go. I suppose my first mistake was going fishing when I should have been working. This was my second mistake, or maybe it was my third, or fourth. I hadn't been keeping a tab on the number, but they seemed to be piling up quickly.

CHAPTER 11

The morning was pretty much history by time I entered the administration building. A clock visible through an open office door said it was five to twelve. Marcie was going to have to settle for lunch, I mused as I hurried along the long, low-ceiling corridor. The place looked as old on the inside as it did from the outside. Overhead, the building's plumbing hung naked from the ceiling. Utilities were simpler back when they built the place. Open the windows on hot summer days, close them in the winter. Rap on the pipes and you got steam, if you were lucky. And air conditioning? Hey, this was Colorado at 6000 feet elevation. Who needed air conditioning? It was only much later that man became more season conscious. Maybe the weather was milder fifty years ago?

When modern heating and cooling needed to be retrofitted, the most expedient course was to hang the plumbing from the ceiling where it was out of the way. The result being an even lower ceiling, which lent a cluttered appearance overhead but was no real inconvenience except perhaps to the occasional basketball star visiting the Office of the Registrar.

The low ceiling with its spaghetti network of exposed pipes painted the same color as the walls reminded me of another set of narrow passageways. They were tighter, with lots of up and down via iron-rung ladders, but the sameness was enough to bring a knot to my stomach. I recalled the constant rumble of pumps and whooshing of ventilation fans, and unlike the nice white paint everything wore here, those passages were painted navy gray.

It had been my first and only time inside a submarine; a hectic seven hours of squeezing down narrow passageways, of waiting in a pretty well-equipped messroom, drinking coffee, listening to soft chatter from the sailors on break, trying to ignore the persistent background noise of one of the more complicated machines ever built. Eventually the brain learned to block most of it out, but at first, after the chopper had lowered us aboard somewhere in the Sea of Japan, the noise, the hiss of compressed air rushing through the pipes overhead, that was all that I was aware of.

By time I started getting used to it, we were breaking surface under a moonless sky. The coast was black and rose and fell as the vessel beneath us rode the waves. The inflatable dinghy was black too and looked like a wet seal. There was barely enough room in it for my partner and me, our gear including the long, hermetically sealed aluminum rifle case, and the two sailors from the boat who rowed us ashore.

I'd never worked with Randall Potter before then—they seldom let operatives get that familiar with each other—but the man made me a little nervous. Randall seemed to be the sort who lived every second as if he had a lit stick of dynamite shoved up his rear end and no idea how much longer the fuse had to burn. He had an unusual affinity for the black rifle resting across his knees, as if it might be a viable substitute for good old fashion common sense. I tried to put the worry out of mind. We were both taut. It's always like that on one of these in-and-out missions.

We got in all right, make the touch—a Vietnamese general named Phan—and left the sniper-scoped Russian Mosin Nagant where it was sure to be found. It all was going as planned and we would have been out of there in a couple hours but for the gook patrol. Randall opened fire on them before I had a chance to raise my hands. He died there in the jungle. I was taken to their command post and interrogated. I would have died too if not for a sleepy guard who was too young and too inexperienced for the job. He died by his own bayonet instead.

I pulled my thoughts back to the present and turned a corner into a wider hall with classrooms one either side and a door to the outside at the far end. And just then, a Saturday class let out and I found myself in the middle of a swarm of young faces heading for the doorway. I shed my coat, tucked it under my arm and joined the crowd. Outside, I veered off hurrying around one of the newer brick buildings. The shade dropped the temperature at least ten degrees and I was shivering when I came around the front corner. The Porsche hadn't moved. Well, I hadn't expected it to leave without us.

I wouldn't exactly say the campus was awash with students heading for their cars, this being Saturday, but the traffic was heavy enough for me to blend in without being noticed now that I wasn't wearing the coat, which after all this time should have been a sign the man in the red car was looking for. As it turned out he wasn't looking for me at all but had his binoculars focused across the parking lot on Marcie and my truck. She had a comb in her hand and I wondered how long she'd been pulling it through her hair. Marcie was quite good at following orders, I decided as slipped the Smith and Wesson from my pocket and leaned into the open window, pressing the cold steel barrel against the neck of the gent inside.

He stiffened and the binoculars crashed against the gearshift knob and bounced onto the floor. "What...?" he yelped.

He was definitely an amateur and he showed it. I said in the most dangerous tone I could muster, "Think twice about your next move, mister. This pistol is resting on your carotid artery. It's a twenty-two and won't make a lot of noise, especially when muffled by skin." I kept the revolver hidden under the coat folded over my arm and fitted an amiable smile on my face just in case anyone cared enough to be watching us. I waved at Marcie over the top of the car. Keeping my voice low and threatening, I said, "Try anything clever or stupid, I'll turn all this pretty beige leather and carpeting red as the outside of this expensive piece of German machinery. Understand?" Sure, I was playing up the drama, but I had a feeling the chubby fellow was susceptible to melodramatics.

He nodded, breathing hard, eyes bulging as if on the verge of a coronary. His neck had gone stiff as concrete and his face was almost as pale. Little beads of sweat pricked his cheeks and forehead. Physiologically speaking, I'd have judged him to be the type who'd have sweat a lot anyway, but now he had more than ample reason to do so. Up close he looked younger than my first impression of him. Probably twenty-eight or thirty. Thick eyebrows gave the impression of age, as did the dated plaid cap, a piece of apparel from an earlier era when driving a sports car involved getting intimate with your car under the hood. He sported a pale blond mustache and jowly, beardless cheeks. He obviously lived a fat, easy life. His face, while presently drained of blood still showed evidence of a rich tan; he'd either been traveling in warmer climes or lounging under sun lamps.

I said, "Turn your head slowly and look at me. Keep in mind I'm an expert marksman. Any foolish heroics and I'll pull this trigger, and there's not a thing you can do to stop me." I was spreading it on pretty thick. I'd never been much of an expert marksman with anything that had a barrel shorter than an M1 Garand...or a Mosin Nagant...but there was no reason he needed to know that.

His head turned in a jerky manner, his eyes widening at the revolver then lifting toward my face. His lower lip fell away from the mustache in surprise.

"You...you're him!" he sputtered, his view leaping to the building I'd entered a few minutes earlier.

A worrisome gnawing began to chew at my stomach. His reaction wasn't right. None of this felt right. It was either a trap or I'd made a huge mistake. I said, "You know who I am?" That was a dumb question. Of course, he'd have been told something about who he was following.

He swallowed hard and nodded, his view fixed on the revolver.

"Then you're one up on me, mister." My pickup truck pulled behind the car and the door squeaked open. His view swung momentarily toward it as Marcie climbed out.

"What are you going to do with that gun?" he asked haltingly.

"Probably shoot you if you don't behave yourself. What do you think I'm going to do with it?" That had been a naive question and I was getting the uneasy feeling. The gent wasn't just an amateur, he wasn't even in the game.

He blinked sweat from his eyes and licked it from his lips. "I won't do anything to provoke you. Please don't point that thing at me."

Marcie stopped alongside me, quietly observant.

I said to him, "I'll decide when to put it away, but first a few questions."

"I'll...I'll tell you whatever you want to know," he stammered.

"Who are you working for?"

"Working?" He seemed genuinely surprised at my question. "I'm not working for anyone." That gnawing in my gut took a big bite and I glanced around hoping we weren't attracting unwanted attention, like from a curious campus cop. I said to Marcie, "Recognize him?"

"No."

I said, "Then why have you been following us?"

He gulped and blinked the shine from his eyes. "I wanted to know who you were, what you were like, what you do." He sounded embarrassed to confessed it.

This was taking a disturbing twist. I began to run through the charges I could be facing. Brandishing a weapon, intimidation, assault. I took a long breath and let it out slowly. "Let me get this straight. You picked us up in Woodland Park and practically sat on my bumper all the way down the mountain just because you wanted to see what I was like? Personal curiosity-?, or is there a point behind this?"

"I had a reason," He said softly. He seemed to be having trouble getting the words out. "I was hoping to get something on you, something I could use against you."

"Against me? Why? For whose benefit?"

He hesitated, lowered his chin to his head, and said regretfully, "My own."

Now I was totally confused. I glanced at Marcie hoping to find some insight there, but she only shrugged, as mystified as I was. I said, "Spell it out, buddy."

He drew a breath and said, "I wanted to get something on you. Something I could use in my defense, okay?" His voice held a sharp note of indignation. "Something I could hold up in front of Sherri to prove you weren't the right guy for her. That I was.

That's why I was following you." He scowled and took in another breath.

Marcie started laughing.

I said, "You're a jealous boyfriend?" I might have shot the guy because he wasn't able to keep his hormones under control. And where would that have left me? In jail. I became keenly aware of the students drifting past us on the way to their cars, doors opening and slamming and engines starting. Fortunately, everyone seemed more interested in getting away for lunch than in two people having a *friendly* conservation with the gent in the expensive car. A van drove past and parked a couple spaces away. A girl and her boyfriend walked past and kept going. So far we hadn't drawn any undue attention.

I lowered the hammer on the revolver and stealthily slipped it into my pocket. Oddly, I was more tense now than before. I'd broken several laws, and I would likely end up in jail if this fellow decided to talk to a lawyer about my socially unacceptable manner of communication. Marcie had stopped laughing, but her face held a silly I-told-you-so grin. I said, "What's your name?"

"Brian Landerfelt," he said forcefully now that he felt he'd gotten the upper hand...and maybe he had."

"Well, Brian, you almost got a bullet in your fool head."

"Yeah? Someone ought to punch you in the nose, mister," he came back with justifiable anger—well, justifiable I guess from his point of view...and maybe it was.

I was about to give him a lecture on the dangers

of following people you don't know when behind me Marcie gave a startled yelp that was cut short. I started to turn when something hard jabbed my ribs. I hadn't paid attention to the van that had pulled into the slot beside us, and now three men moved in tight around us. A glance at Marcie's deer-in-the-headlights eyes told me she knew these men.

I recognized one of them too.

CHAPTER 12

The van was a big, shiny, custom job with tinted windows, thick carpeting and deep, furry captain's seats—two up front, two in the center, and three in back where Marcie, Landerfelt and I'd been put. The seats appeared to be quite comfortable, but I had no way of knowing that with my hands tied behind my back and the rope secured to the bottom frame of the seat. Not exactly a comfortable position.

To my right was Landerfelt, sitting in a similarly awkward position, now and then giving forth a low whimper and a sniffle. Maybe he was thinking about what *Pretty Boy* had done to his expensive upholstery and sheet metal. Pretty Boy was the name I'd given the one with the pistol, styled hairdo, leather western sports coat, fancy ostrich cowboy boots with the high heels. The outfit made him look kind of feminine. It almost made me wonder about his bed mate preferences, but the way he'd manhandled Marcie into the van, his hands wandering as he'd done so, suggested otherwise.

On my left sat Marcie; straight back, defiant chin, burning glare drilling holes through Pretty Boy in the row ahead of us. He held a 1911 .45 over the top of the seat as if seriously suspecting one of us might be a Houdini in disguise. Marcie wasn't the least intimidated.

I managed to catch her eye. Her glance didn't linger long, but in that moment, there was an exchange of sorts that chilled my blood. I'd recognized something smoky and unreadable in those blue eyes, a ruthlessness I'd seen a time or two in the past—in the eyes of men who knew what had to be done and that likely they wouldn't be coming home. I'd noted that same look last night on the hill above the restaurant; a determination that drives a person to beat unconquerable odds or die trying. And I knew then that everything she'd told me an hour ago had been just another lie. I grimaced, strangely enough not at all surprised.

I was relieved that at the moment her hands were tied, or we might have a real mess right here, inside the van, in the middle of Academy Boulevard.

The driver, Alexander, looked over his shoulder at us. His eyes were brown, flecked with yellow. They watched us a moment then turned back to the road. Like Landerfelt, he was a beefy fellow, but beneath the plaid hunting shirt, sleeves turned up to his elbows, was muscle, not adipose. He'd been one of the men behind the restaurant last night, and earlier the man in my rearview mirror swinging a hunting rifle toward the tailgate of my bounding truck. Outdoor living had darkened his face. He needed a shave...but then I was beginning to look a little like Gabby Hayes myself.

The fellow in the seat beside him was taller but half the weight. His eyes were set deep beneath the overhang of a bony brow-ridge topped with a caterpillar-shag of dark hair. Above the eyebrows his forehead jutted up and curved smoothly back onto a hairless pate rimmed in a tangled wreath that may have never felt the tug of a comb—well, at least that was the impression. His ears were small and his nose suggested a lineage traceable back to Sherlock Holmes. A jutting chin was made more pronounced by the dagger of hair at its end. He appeared a cheerless fellow, never speaking, ever cerebrating.

And then there was Pretty Boy who enjoyed slashing leather automobile seats and dragging metal objects across shiny red paint. The high heel of his fancy cowboy boot had put a dandy dent in Brian Landerfelt's door too as we were being escorted away. Pretty Boy gave the impression of a man who took long walks after a rainfall just to squish earthworms on the sidewalk. He had a fetish for combs, touching women's breasts, and studying his reflection in car windows. I gleaned all this in the few moments it took to move us from Landerfelt's car into the van's open side door.

They'd moved in on us quickly, surrounding us to keep the eyes of passing students from seeing or suspecting too much. Just a bunch of guys and a pretty gal in an oversize coat having a friendly chit-chat.

"You've been making life unpleasant for all of us, my dear," The man in the plaid shirt had said to Marcie.

Marcie'd been momentarily knocked off stride. It didn't take long to recover. Her eyes narrowed darkly. "You're breaking my heart, Alexander. Wouldn't want you to take heat on my account." She fixed a sarcastic grin to her lips with not a trace of the fear I knew she was keeping a tight rein on. Good ol' blood thirsty Marcie Rose! She squared her shoulders and hip-planted her hands in a defiant show of bravado. "You're not waving around any guns. Did they take them away from you, or do you think Jeffy here has the balls to handle the hardware?"

Pretty boy took a menacing step toward her raising the automatic. Her words must have triggered something inside him because he didn't seem to care if anyone there in the university parking saw the gun. Alexander stepped between them. "Put that down!"

Pretty Boy hesitated, then jabbed the pistol hard into my back to show how tough he really was. I winced and made another tick on the mental score card I was keeping inside my head. I'd settle up when the time was right. Pretty Boy was as shade taller than me, built something along the lines of a bowling pin with the widest point being the seat of his designer western style trousers held up by a stitched and carved leather belt and silver rodeo buckle. I'd have given five to ten he'd never forked a saddle and couldn't rope a bull if his life depended on it, let alone wrestle one to the ground.

Alexander took a breath when the troops settled down and looked at Marcie. "This is hardly the place to renew old antagonisms," he said. "Jeff is quite capable of handling all the firearms that we'll be needing for the three of you."

The hawk-beaked man—I figured him as the

one named Raymond who Marcie had mentioned earlier—moved closer to Landerfelt and removed a hand from his long trench coat pocket and showed him a tiny pistol. Probably a .25 or .22. A Colt Junior from the brief glimpse I'd gotten of it. He slipped it back out of sight. The exercise was probably unnecessary seeing as Sherri's spurned lover was not in any emotional condition to even think about fleeing. He hadn't yet fully recovered from staring into the barrel of my revolver, which was still resting reassuringly in my pocket.

"Of course, it's not," Marcie was saying. "Too many eyes make you nervous. A lonely mountain cabin is more to your liking."

Alexander grinned and rubbed the material of her baggy parka between his thumb and finger and said, "Torrance's coat. Somewhat large for you, wouldn't you say?" He shook his head. "Torrance was a good man."

"He got in my way," she replied flatly.

Alexander's expression hardened. "I'll keep that in mind." He glanced around the parking lot, students moving purposefully toward cars or the busy highway crossing where many of them had parked along neighborhood streets. "We've wasted enough time here." He said to the man in the trench coat. "I suspect the gentleman is carrying. See to it that he's relieved of the temptation to die early. Don't forget to retrieve the transmitter, too."

The man found the revolver and moved it from my pocket to his own. I hated to lose it but I didn't really expect it to go unnoticed. Jeff and Alexander had escorted us to the van while the man ducked beneath the back bumper of my truck and came up holding a small, black box that must have been outfitted with a magnet...

The van hit a pothole, jolting my thoughts back to the present. The .45 was still pointed at us, but Jeff seemed to be getting bored. Well, there really wasn't much activity going on back here. Each of us was occupied with our own thoughts. Brian was dealing with a case of mild terror while Marcie, I'm pretty sure, was thinking murderous thoughts. Good ol' bloodthirsty Marcie Rose.

I said, "Just out of curiosity, how long has my truck been wired?" The question wasn't directed at anyone in particular. Alexander answered, not taking his view from the road. Probably studiously avoiding potholes, of which Colorado Springs seemed to have more than its fair share of.

"We tagged you at the restaurant. After you got away down that goat trail of a road back in the mountains, I couldn't afford to lose you again. I got your numbers but it was an out of state plate and it would have taken too much time to run you down through regular channels."

I said, "You could have taken us anytime? Why did you wait until now?"

"Almost anytime. There're hundreds of dirt tracks in those mountains and you could have been on any one of them. We had the transmitter's signal but it took time to narrow it down to a searchable area, and it was morning before we located the cabin. Because we didn't know how well armed you were, and since bullets won't penetrate a log structure, we elected to wait and take you coming out...but there were complications."

I smiled. "A complication driving a cream-colored Mercedes."

Landerfelt gasped and gave me a startled look that told me he hadn't known Sherri'd been to the cabin. That meant she hadn't driven back down the pass to the Springs or he would have seen her too. There was always the chance he'd missed her car since it was my truck he was looking for, but I'd call that a long shot.

I said, "You could have moved in after she left."

Alexander confirmed my suspicion. "We decided to see to the young lady first. We didn't know what she'd been told." He cast an accusatory glance at Marcie who murdered him with her stare. "We'd have moved in on you sooner if your partner here hadn't been covering the back door."

Landerfelt gave a startled look. Well, it was an understandable mistake for Alexander to make from the evidence at hand.

Alexander continued, glancing over his shoulder at Landerfelt, "That was clever, keeping just enough distance between you and him that if one got hit the other could make his getaway." He returned his attention to the road. "We considered making our move back there at STE but waited until we could get the three of you together."

He had his neatly tied-up explanation that covered the facts as he imagined them. I couldn't see any useful reason to correct him. At a stop light a car ahead of us wore the bumper sticker: *Pray for me, I drive Academy.*

I said, "What did you do with her?"

Marcie was watching me. Maybe she just wanted to see my reaction?

Pretty Boy said, "You'll find out soon enough."

Alexander said, "She's unharmed—so far. We're all going to go someplace nice and private where we can talk about it."

Marcie shivered. She'd been to one of their talks and it had left an impression.

Landerfelt's lips trembled. He understood the implication. Well, he had nothing of value to talk about, and for that matter, neither did I. All I needed to do was convince Alexander of that or there was going to be a real mess to clean up, and I didn't think either of us would be in any condition to be doing any cleaning. I could hold out a long time under heavy persuasion; I'd been worked on by experts in that field a time or two in the past. But when you have nothing to give there isn't much point in keeping you around. I was pretty sure Alexander *et al.* had no intentions of allowing any of us to go free.

Thinking it over, trying to convince them that we did know something might be a helpful tactic. If only Marcie had told me something useful!

On the padded engine cover between Raymond and Alexander lay my Smith and Wesson, I noted wryly. Being all trussed up like a bulldogged calf, and with Jeff waiting for a chance to go bang-bang with that .45, the little revolver might as well have been back at the cabin locked in a drawer.

The situation was taking on an uncomfortable deja vu. Another time, another place. Slant-eyed faces scowling at me. Arms lashed to a bamboo chair under a hot sun in a sweltering land. The faces never smiled. They just waited...waited patiently for the heat and humidity to draw out the answers to their questions. Now and then they'd prod me with the point of a bayonet, ask their questions again, and then let the roasting heat do its job. At least I'd been supplied a cover story and managed to give believable responses one after another as the questions had been asked in broken English. I pretended not to understand the words they spoke back and forth to each other.

The lies had worked well enough to buy me time, to eventually find myself alone one rainy night with a sleepy guard who'd made the mistake of becoming careless with his seemingly complacent charge. I'd covered his mouth and plunged the blade of his own knife hard and deep. I recalled the effort it took to yank it free from where it lodged between bone and tough heart muscle. The dark, the rain, the bamboo walls and a sleepy guard all worked in my favor.

I wasn't going to kid myself that making my escape from Alexander and his crew was going to be as successful.

CHAPTER 13

When the van turned off Academy onto Fountain Boulevard, I was pretty sure where we were going. I'd flown into Colorado Springs once, a few years ago, and my brother had come down from his cabin to pick me up. It was a couple miles to the airport, past large, industrial buildings, and down a narrow access road to a row of private hangars on the north end of the civilian side of the runways. The Colorado Springs Municipal Airport shares runways with the Air Force over on the Peterson Field side. Alexander parked between two corrugated steel hangars, behind Sherri's Mercedes. Jeff slid the side door open and stepped down to the asphalt, brandishing the pistol for God and everyone to see, but we'd parked in a pretty secluded spot. Alexander came back with a pocketknife and sliced the ropes anchoring us to the seat frames.

I came out first squinting in the bright light, the severed end of the rope dangling from my still tied wrists and raised my hands against the glare off the shiny steel buildings. Jeff waved me toward an open door. I didn't think much of Pretty Boy and the more I saw of him, the more I figured him for an insecure lightweight. Pistol or no, I was pretty sure I could take him even with my hands tied but this wasn't the time to try it. The only real cover I had was the main terminal building on the other side of the wide runway, too far away to attempt a foot race against a bullet.

I glanced at Raymond, his hand in his pocket. I was pretty sure it gripped the little Colt pistol. I didn't have much faith in the tiny .25's usefulness. In a pinch it was marginally better than a clenched fist, I supposed. At the very least a pistol, any pistol, is a great psychological deterrent. No sensible person wanted to be perforated with a bunch of bleeding holes, even if they were little holes. As for stopping power, the diminutive caliber was several notches below what's considered marginal, right down there with the venerable .22. Only a fool would carry one as serious protection, or someone who knows little about guns...apologies to Ian Fleming's famous spy.

It was warm inside the dim hangar. After a few moments my eyes adjusted to the gloom. It wasn't really all that dark here, it just seemed so at first. Overhead a bank of fluorescent tubes illuminated a low-winged twin engine aircraft with a rolling set of aluminum stair steps had been pushed up to the open door. A mechanic had one of the engine's cowlings off and his head and arms poked inside the innards.

I'm not all that familiar with planes, but this one looked to be very expensive, very high class. Judging from the number of windows along the fuselage, I guessed it carried six to eight passengers in comfort.

Raymond shut the hangar door and locked it. Alexander cut the rope binding our wrists. "Any theatrics and the ropes go back on." We weren't going anywhere, and he knew it.

Marcie shed her coat and looked the place over. The old shirt I'd given her to wear was baggy but not so much so as to hide the fact that she was a woman. Involuntarily I recalled undressing her the night before when I'd put her to bed, and suddenly I wanted her. I was thinking about Sherri too. Physically speaking, Sherri had more to offer, but I had a feeling that when it came down to using what each had been endowed with, Marcie would be in the major leagues while Sherri would be still working her way up through the minors. Maybe that was unfair. I had, after all, no evidence to support the conclusion, and anyway, this was a hell of a time to be thinking about sex.

I pulled my thoughts back to the situation at hand. The hangar held only the six of us, and the mechanic who'd glanced over his shoulder when we'd entered and then had gone back to his engine. A dark movement through one of the small windows caught my eye.

"You're worried about her," Marcie said quietly as Alexander strolled to the plane and spoke to the mechanic. Her face held an intense look and I wondered how long she'd been studying me like that. Had she sensed my earlier thoughts? I almost felt guilty—but not so much knowing that I'd probably take her up on her offer of the night before should it be made again.

Marcie nodded toward the airplane. "She's in there."

"I know."

"I'm sorry she got involved, Granger." Marcie winced. "It's becoming...complicated." I had a feeling she was sincere this time. "It's all my fault," she continued.

I said, "Forget it. This isn't the time or place for sentiments." The last thing I needed was for Marcie to go soft on me, not that I thought there was much chance of that happening.

She gave a grin, but her eyes were still frowning. "Mr. Tall Guy with a heart of flint. I only hope you're as tough as you pretend to be when they put the thumb screws to you."

I did too and tried not to let my thoughts go there. And then Landerfelt crashed into us sending us staggering. I grabbed for Marcie but she was already heading for the concrete floor. Pretty Boy jabbed Landerfelt in the stomach with the automatic and kicked Marcie out of his way with a pointy-toe boot. Landerfelt cowed, covering his face with his hands while trying to protect his middle with his elbows. Pretty Boy Jeff laughed at Landerfelt's clumsy attempt to protect himself and poked him again with the pistol.

"When I tell you to move, I mean MOVE!" Pretty Boy said in his best James Cagney voice, glowering like a street-corner bully who'd just corralled the neighborhood sissy, a *real* man with a big gun in his hand. "Hey, look at me, fatso!" He poked Landerfelt again just for the fun of it, a curl on his lips that would have made Mephistopheles look downright saintly. I didn't like what I was seeing.

"I said look at me!" Pretty Boy snarled.

But Brian Landerfelt was busy hiding behind his arms, too frozen from fright by the sudden attack to be comply. That only made Pretty Boy angrier. The kid had a temper problem. His eyes glared savagely, and his voice rose, accusing Landerfelt of having an incestuous relationship with his mother although not exactly in those words. Without any warning at all, Pretty Boy hammered the pistol into Landerfelt's mouth. Landerfelt cried out and stumbled back, blood running through his fingers. Pretty Boy went after him like a hungry shark. Landerfelt stumbled over a toolbox and hit the floor hard.

Raymond stood nearby scowling. Alexander and the mechanic had looked over from the plane. They didn't appear pleased with the performance, but no one had made an effort to break it up. Pretty Boy struck with those pointy boots again, aiming for a groin shot but missing, his face a crimson glow, the snarl on his lips pure hate. As if it could get much worse, the scene turned ugly. Pretty Boy racked the slide of the pistol back, ejecting a perfectly good shell and feeding in a fresh one. Maybe he did it on purpose to further terrify Landerfelt, but I suspected rage had overcome rational thinking and he didn't realize the gun already had a bullet in the chamber.

And still no one did anything to try and stop it. I didn't owe Landerfelt anything, but the kid with the stiletto boots had racked up a list of offenses that I had intended to settle up on sometime soon. It's funny how a notion comes from seemingly out of nowhere and takes hold. It may be a dumb-ass idea, the kind that ends up getting you killed, but it sets its teeth and there's no letting go.

I moved in with a low, quick fist to the kid's stomach. Air exploded from his lungs and the pistol skittered away someplace. I didn't care where. It wasn't on my radar. I came up with a short jab to his chin. Pretty Boy's head snapped back and then suddenly I had it in a particular hold I hadn't used in over twenty years, hadn't even thought about it, but there it was. Reflexes took over; pressure to the neck vertebrae, a twist to his chin, and the sharp snap that told me I'd properly executed the maneuver. The kid went limp...and then the hangar went psychedelic. I glimpsed a warped, hall-of-mirrors image of Alexander standing with something long and black raising up over his head. The black thing swung downward and the grotesque image winked out, and all went black.

CHAPTER 14

Somewhere in the vicinity of my forehead an infer-
no blazed.

A low, far away murmuring faintly seeped into
my consciousness. Much closer a persistent vibra-
tion pushed waves of motion up my spine, crashing
into fire raging behind my eyes. The sensation was
quite unpleasant and I felt I might retch if it continued too much longer.

I'd begun the long stead crawl to consciousness
whether I wanted too or not. Frankly, I wasn't too
thrilled with the prospect of facing the pain straight
on with eyes wide open. The climb came in stages,
and with each advance my peripheral awareness
improved and the fire in my head burned hotter.
My hands, I discovered, had been tied again. Well, I
couldn't blame them. I had acted rather unsociable
once they'd been untied, and Alexander had warned
me of the consequences. Beneath me was a rough
texture, which I recognized as cloth upholstery as
one might find in a car or truck...or an airplane.

Something cold and damp pressed against my forehead. Something soft and gentle stroked my temple. Something like the scent of lilacs reached my nose.

Consciousness arrived with a tremendous stabbing of pain between my eyes, which I kept screwed shut against the light—natural light not artificial. How did I know that?

"I think he's coming around." That was Alexander.

"Too bad," An unfamiliar voice replied.

"Paul? Paul, can you hear me?"

I forced open an eye. Her pale, washed-out features were out of focus. "Sherri," I murmured.

"I'm here, Paul." Sudden relief eased some of the tension in her face. The corners of her lips hitched up in an effort to smile. "Oh, Paul, we've been so worried about you." Her words sounded strained.

"Speak for yourself, lady?" Came that same voice from the front of the plane.

Sherri scowled at the man behind the controls.

I tried to sit up. A hot iron struck me between the eyes driving me back against the reclined seat. Sherri said, "Don't move, darling. Rest a little while longer."

It occurred to me that I hadn't heard Marcie's voice, and I didn't know if what I was feeling was curiosity or worry. "Help me sit up. How do you work this damned thing?" I said groping double-handed for the button or lever that normally resides somewhere on an airplane armrest.

Sherri disapproved, but her hand left my shoulder and a moment later the seat back rose, Sherri restraining it so that it didn't lift too quickly. "How's that, Paul? Do you need a pillow?"

"You're treating him like a baby," Marcie said harshly. The sound of her voice lifted a small amount of the worry I felt. She came from behind me, took my wrist to check my pulse and then peered into my face, lifting an eyelid with a thumb, first the left and then the right, coming to the conclusion that I didn't have a concussion and all I really needed were a couple aspirins. "Well, where are they?" Marcie demanded, louder this time because no one had paid any attention to her. "I know you've got a first aid kit aboard."

Alexander, seated in front of us, facing us, pointed to the rear of the plane with Pretty Boy's pistol. I glanced down the center aisle. Landerfelt was in the row behind us, but Pretty Boy was not aboard. Marcie made her way aft. I said to Alexander, "Where's the kid?"

"You did him good, Granger."

"Dead?"

"No, but he'll wish he was. He won't be walking again. He can breathe on his own, but not much more."

"Where is he?"

"Hospital," Alexander said.

"How'd you explain it?"

He shrugged. "Accidents happen when you work around machinery. The officials bought it okay." His voice hardened. "I don't like having to explain bodies, Granger. I'll be sure we won't have that problem with yours."

I said, "Then you'll have to do a better job of packaging it up than you did with Carl." It was a shot in the dark but it must have hit something.

Alexander stiffened slightly, his view narrowing. "What do you know about that?"

The thing is, I knew nothing but what little Marcie had said, and I'd wager maybe ninety percent of that had been lies, but if I was going to convince them I had information worth keeping alive a little while longer, now was as good a time as any to begin talking.

I said, "He found out what you were up to and didn't like it. He told Marcie and a few others. I heard this from a third party," I added cryptically to give them something to more to worry about."

Marcie appeared at my side with a plastic glass of water and she dumped two aspirins into my hand. Her view was narrow and not friendly. "You talk too much, Granger." She knew the game I was playing.

Sherri's mouth had gaped, her eyes wore a confused. "What's going on here, Paul?"

I ignored her, watching Alexander chew his lower lip. "Who told you that?" he demanded.

"I told him," Marcie intervened haltingly and not very convincingly.

He glanced over, then back. "Make it easy on yourself, Granger. Give me a name and maybe I can talk the boss into letting up on some of the heat."

That got the pilot's attention and he looked over his shoulder at the back of Alexander's head. His suit coat hung on a hook behind his seat and I saw how his belly strained the buttons of his shirt. Little crescents of sweat soaked the cloth at his armpits. His brown hair was going gray and his face clean shaven. A cigarette drooped from his lips and bobbed convulsively with his small, quiet laugh.

"Don't listen to him, Granger," Marcie glared at the pilot. "What about it, Cockran? You going to let your peons make the deals?"

I hadn't pictured Sten Cockran like that. Somehow, I thought there'd be something sinister about the man, something overtly dangerous in his appearance. Instead, he reminded me of a dentist I used to go to.

Cockran grinned around the cigarette that danced in his lips as he spoke. "I don't care who makes the deals Miss Rose, so long as I get what I'm after." It was the unidentified voice that had spoken earlier, and it sounded reasonably pragmatic now. Sten Cockran was plainly a practical man.

Sherri said, "Someone tell me what's going on here." She'd never been one to shrink quietly into the background for very long. Sure, everything that had happened had put her back on her high heels, who wouldn't have been knocked off their stride, but now that the shock had lost its rough edges Sherri was damn well going have some answers. "I'm run off the road, kidnapped, and taken to that grimy airplane garage. Brian is assaulted, Paul's head almost split open, and now we are a mile in the air heading to who knows where!" Her view swept the cabin falling on me. "Tell me what's happening, Paul."

I said, "I don't know. Honestly, I don't. Why don't you ask the man with the gun?"

Sherri looked at Alexander. "Well, you going to tell me?"

Landerfelt stirred in the seat next row back, plainly interested in hearing the answer too. Well, that made three of us. I was pretty sure Marcie knew where we were going, but she wasn't talking.

"Sit down, lady," Alexander said, waving the pistol

threateningly like Pretty Boy had been wont to do. Maybe guns did that to certain people, people who didn't use them often enough to know that sometimes they go bang when you didn't expect them to? Accidents happen. They've happened to me and to friends of mine. If you're lucky no one gets hurt and you've learned a lesson safe gun handling you're not likely to forget.

Sherri sank wide-eyed quietly into the seat across the aisle from me. Alexander was bluffing but Sherri didn't know that. He'd not fire a gun inside an airplane at altitude. I didn't know how high we were flying, but it appeared to be a lot more that the "mile" Sherri had called it; high enough to have a pressurized hull, which a .45 slug would quickly and violently depressurize, not to mention the possibility of severing cables, hydraulic lines, or electrical wires.

Below us stretched the brown bowl of a valley rimmed with mountains. We were flying into the sun. Craning my neck—with much accompanying pain—I looked back along the fuselage at the profile of Pikes Peak. That would make the valley we were flying over South Park. Cattle country now. Indian land a hundred and fifty years ago. Sunlight sparkled off a long, narrow patch of blue water that was Eleven Mile Reservoir. I'd fished the stream below the dam a couple times.

Alexander said to me, "We'll talk later."

I shrugged. "What good will it do me?"

"We'll make a deal, maybe."

And if I believed that I'm sure he had a bridge somewhere he'd be happy to sell me. "Maybe," I said glancing at Cockran who'd returned his attention to flying the plane. In the copilot seat Raymond pondered a chart. He hadn't partaken in the activities back here. He either didn't care or was too occupied with navigating to concern himself with a couple of women and men who weren't going anywhere until their feet were firmly back on solid ground.

Marcie had taken the seat behind me, which faced toward the rear of the plane and two more seats that faced forward, a small table between them. Sherri had gone quiet, staring at the automatic Alexander had lowered to his lap.

"I wish you would tell me what's going on, Paul," she said quietly.

"I wish I could," I said. She looked annoyed, as if I was holding something back from her on purpose.

"Really, Paul, if this is a joke it's gone on long enough."

That startled me. Is that what she thought of all this? A joke? Then I realized that in the beginning it must have seemed that way to her. Someone was playing a nasty joke on her, and now it was all going to end. How could sweet, protected, Sherri Lane have thought otherwise? She'd grown up in the shadows of the Broadmoor Hotel, in the safe confines of Daddy's walled estate that Granddad had built from Cripple Creek gold at the end of the last century.

Was this the first, honest taste Sherri ever had of life in the real world? If so, life had just played a dirty trick on her, I mused, and maybe it was a wake-up call the young lady needed. Now, if only I could make sure she survived long enough to benefit from the experience.

CHAPTER 15

We flew low over a couple picturesque mountain villages, the sun on the horizon, setting behind snow covered mountain peaks spiking toward a darkening sky. During our slow descent Sherri had turned in her seat and spoke to Landerfelt. I think it was the first time since I'd regained consciousness that she'd said more than a half dozen words to the fellow.

"How did you get all mixed up in this, Brian?" Her voice was low, but I heard disapproval in it.

He winced and looked embarrassed. "I could ask you the same question."

She scowled briefly, then her expression softened. "I'm sorry, Brian." She glanced my way with disapproval. "I can guess how we both got involved."

He said, "It's my fault, not his, but I was doing it for you, Sherri. I had to do something; don't you see? I couldn't just give you up. Don't you see?"

"For me? Or for you?" Her lips compressed drawing an unattractive line across her face. "We've been through this," she said.

"I know, but-"

"But you didn't listen. I might as well have been talking to my horse." The anger in her eyes softened a bit. "We aren't children anymore. We had wonderful times growing up and all, but that's past. I've changed... you've changed. We were great friends, but that's all it was. That's all it will ever be. Can't you see that?"

"Why must it be only that? Because I'm not one of those causes you find yourself drawn to? Because our fathers happen to be business partners? Why, Sherri? Why can't it work for us?" His voice cracked, his eyes taking on a sheen. He sat back in the seat and turned his head to the window. It wasn't the scenery he cared about, but he had enough self-respect to not want to display his tears.

Sherri was dealing with emotions too, not concerned who might notice the drop of moisture from her pooling eyes. "Oh Brian, if only you'd understand," she said. She smiled briefly at me and then looked to the darkening landscape below slowly rising toward us.

Lights strung along ski lifts were winking on, dropping pale yellowish pools on the snow-covered slopes. The illumination accentuated the deep darkness of the pine forests from which the runs had been hacked out of. The plane banked low over a small village all lit up like Christmas. The season still had a couple more months to go, depending on how much snow spring brought. Some of the more expensive ski slopes used snow makings machines to extend the season. We leveled off and headed out over the forest, dropping steadily. A lighted runway appeared beyond the tops of the trees. Landing gears lowered with a muted electric whine and gave a solid clunk locking in place. Beyond the runway, among the trees, was a house with lots of bright windows and at least two patios alit. The forest dropped away and a strip of asphalt rose up to kiss the plane's tires, and we were down.

Marcie made a point of being the first of us off the plane. She swept past me in a rush, that bulky parka under her arm, her eyes blue lasers fixed on the open door. There were no steps here. Marcie grasped a grab bar and hopped down to the pavement into the fading light of an early winter's evening. Raymond had already deplaned and was waiting on the tarmac with his little pistol in hand.

Landerfelt was next. His face looked a mess, blue and black from Pretty Boy's attack blossoming purple and black. Alexander waved him toward the door with the .45. Landerfelt held the bar, hesitated, and then jumped. He landed on a patch of ice and fell to his knees, his glasses flying off into a pile of slush at Raymond's feet. Raymond fished them out of the cold melt, shook them off and handed them back. Landerfelt said a quiet, "Thank you," and re-placed them on the bridge of his nose making the fine adjustments with the tip of a finger.

Sherri helped me to the door. I still wasn't steady on my feet, and hoping to avoid Landerfelt's fate, sat on the threshold. I could have made it without help, but playing up my poor, shaky state might work to my advantage if they thought my condition worse than it was. I made the trip to the tarmac without drama and double-handed helped Sherri do the same.

This was skiing country. It was colder here, wherever here was. I was pretty sure we'd landed a couple thousand feet higher than from where we'd taken off. I wished I could have put my coat on, but Alexander wasn't taking any more chances, so I accepted my predicament as it was and put up with shivering. I didn't think I'd be outside too long. Alexander made it to the tarmac in one long stretch, turned to say something to Cockran still inside the plane, then waved the pistol toward a glow of lights beyond the dark trees. "That way."

Heavy snowflakes were beginning to fall. Raymond took the lead along a footpath stomped into the snow. I suspected there was a paved walk somewhere beneath the snow, but no one had taken the effort to shovel it. We passed a steel hangar with a decrepit Willys pickup truck parked alongside it next to an odd looking contraption that resembled something from Dr. Moreau's island; a gene splice between an overgrown sled and an airplane, with only the propeller and tail fin of the plane making it through the graft intact.

Sherri kept between me and Landerfelt as if not knowing which one of us she wanted to be closer to. I, as she may be thinking, was not the nice, safe college professor she'd mistaken me for while the respectable Mr. Brian Landerfelt had pretty much proven his affection for her, clumsily as it turned out, but sincere, nonetheless. Marcie paid none of us any attention, her head slowly turning, scanning, eyes searching, brain planning, body taut like a cat in dog country.

The path ended—as most paths usually do. This one terminated at a single, wide step that stretched across at least half the length of a wide, paved porch. A wall was of natural stone and was pierced by a pair of heavy wooden doors flanked by stained glass windows and a pair of heavy, wrought iron porch lights. The windows cast colored light across the terra-cotta tile beneath our feet. Brighter overhead lights snapped on as Raymond approached the door, which opened before he reached it.

We followed him inside; the terra-cotta continuing inside too and spreading out, paving a long, wide room furnished with thick furniture scattered about in cozy, conversational units. An inviting fireplace blazed at the far end of the room with tall windows on either side.

The doorman stepped back as we entered and the first thing I noticed was that the sleeves of white shirt were too short for his arms, but then any shirt sleeve would have been if not specially tailored for him. Sherri gasped and looked away. Marcie eyed him unmoved by his appearance.

The man suffered from giantism. The correct scientific term for the condition is acromegaly. It's caused by an overactive pituitary gland secreting too much growth hormone. I'd read somewhere that the record height for a "giant" was somewhere around nine feet. This fellow wasn't about to break the record, but he did have all the classic symptoms of the disease: Baseball mitt hands, huge feet, jutting jaw, thick nose and an armor-plated brow ridge. He stood with a slight forward bend probably due to some spinal deformation. Even so, he topped me by a good twelve inches, and peered down at us with muddy eyes. A nervous twitch afflicted his cheek. I had the feeling the role of doorman was not his normal job as he seemed tense standing there.

Other rooms and hallways opened onto this Great Room. I couldn't determine how far the house extended in either direction, but this was definitely the focal point. Alexander glanced out the door we'd just entered by, then gave Raymond a nod. Raymond slipped his baby pistol into a pocket and strode to one of the rooms to our right. Alexander moved us to one of the conversational units near the fireplace.

"Very nice," I said looking around.

Alexander fished out a roll of candy from a pocket and said," Yeah, isn't it. You'll get to see more of the place. There's a heated pool out back."

Sherri sat in the chair next to Landerfelt. Marcie slouched in the chair next to mine, legs stretched out and crossed, feet keeping a fast rhythm to whatever beat was playing in her head, or maybe it was just pent-up energy needing to be released.

I said, "Who owns it?"

Alexander grinned. "It's for sure not me." He wasn't giving out any information, but it didn't hurt to try.

The front door opened and Cockran came in, casting a glance our way as he headed for the same room Raymond had gone into. He wore one of those quilted down jackets over his suit coat and looked as if he'd rather have been almost anywhere else than here.

I looked at Alexander. "A war council?"

"Something like that."

"Who's the big chief?"

"That's none of your business."

I said, "Why keep it a secret? You know as well as I none of us is going to leave here alive." That might be either a true or false statement, and Alexander's reaction to it would give me the answer I was fishing for. Actually, I thought the answer was pretty obvious. Just the same, I wanted to hear it from him.

Landerfelt, however, apparently had it figured differently. Maybe he was holding onto the hope that the Feds, or Superman would arrive in the final scene. My words landed on him like Dorothy's house and something snapped.

"No!" he cried leaping from the chair faster than I'd have imagined a man of his bulk could have moved. Wagging his head at the impossibility of the idea he broke in a panic toward the front door, running blindly into the seven-foot doorman's outstretched arms. All of his two hundred plus pounds of him came to an abrupt halt as if he'd just run into the side of Hoover Dam. The doorman took Landerfelt's shoulder in a giant paw, turned him roughly and gave a shove that sent Landerfelt tumbling over the arm of his recently vacated chair.

Sherri leaped to his defense. "You leave Brian alone," she declared comically waving both clenched fists at the deformed giant.

The doorman laughed soundlessly, twisted teeth showing past his fibrillating upper lip. He took a menacing step toward her. She quickly retreated. Alexander said, "Back in your chair, lady."

"You have no right to treat us this way!" Sherri has this thing about rights. Everything had rights:

Men, women, canines, bovines, fish...earth worms probably, although I don't ever recall her mentioning them specifically. She was a bandwagon-jumper. I suspect a guilt deeply buried in her soul made up much of the compulsion, having been born into a pedigree that went back to million dollar gold mines, banking, and now a string of fast-food franchises popping up across the country. I won't say I understood what drove Sherri, but I could see how fighting windmills might be her way to make amends for the double-sixes a cosmic hand had rolled for her in this game called life.

"I said sit down!"

"You're a horrible man," she shot back. Coming from Sherri, that was practically a declaration of war.

Alexander showed her the back of his hand. Sherri retreated, glaring hotly at him, and then turned to Landerfelt. "Are you all right, Brian?"

While all this was going on, Marcie had leaned toward me and whispered, "You know what you're doing, Granger?"

"I think so."

"How about a hint?"

Alexander was still facing Sherri. I said, "Keep on like you're mad as hell at me. Like I'm going to reveal some deep, dark secret and you're going to try and stop me. I'll stall them with a story that will take a little time to check out. Only problem is, I don't know anything of value to them." I slid my view and caught her eye. "You've been stringing me along from the beginning. That was okay at first, but now I need something real. The truth would be nice." I kept my voice low while still emphasizing that last word.

She didn't have any choice. The situation had escalated way beyond how it'd begun. Her view moved off my face, her teeth clenching her lower lip.

"Marcie," I urged beneath my breath.

"The detonators, the RD-35s I told you about? Carl learned what Cockran was doing to them; how he *fixed* them. Altered one component-"

Alexander wheeled and swung the big pistol toward us. "You two! No talking."

Marcie straightened in her chair, glaring at me, and said loudly, "Damned coward. You'd sell your mother for a ticket out of here. You turn my stomach."

Sherri looked at us, startled at Marcie's words.

"What are you looking at, bitch," Marcie spat, and then to Alexander, "You going to make me stay here in the same room with this SOB?"

"Deal with it. I've got problems of my own," Alexander shot back.

Marcie put on a pretty good show. No way of knowing if Alexander had bought into her faux anger. Maybe she'd been an actress in a former career? I'm pretty sure if she wanted me to believe so, she could fabricate a convincing enough story to back it up. I only hoped I could come up with something convincing too. *Fixed them? Fixed them how?* What was she about to tell me? Several possibilities occurred to me at once, but I was only guessing. He fixed them not to detonate? To detonate prematurely? Maybe some kind of tracking implant? He had managed to plant one of those on my truck.

Like I said, I was guessing. Marcie had said some of the devices were shipped to Rocky Flats Arsenal for testing. If Cockran had *fixed them*, how could he slip a *fix* past the military inspectors and testers?

Footsteps sounded on the tile floor, pulling me from my speculations. Cockran came up, exhaled hard and wiped his sweaty brow with a handkerchief. "They give you any trouble?" He asked Alexander, removing a gold cigarette case from his pocket and sticking a smoke between his lips. Marcie eyed the cigarette with something like a hungry desperation in her eyes.

"Nothing I couldn't handle."

Cockran lit the cigarette and slipped the lighter into a pocket. "He wants them downstairs. Louis will give you a hand. You can have Raymond if you think you'll need him; we can't afford to lose them again." He'd made a point of emphasizing that last jab.

Alexander's knuckles whitened around the pistol grip. "Stow it, Cockran."

A smile thinned out around the cigarette between his lips. Why, I wondered, was he making a point of needling Alexander? He turned to the giant. "Go with them."

Louis nodded his bony head.

Alexander scowled but didn't push back against Cockran. It was plain who was the alpha dog in this pack, but I was pretty sure those dynamics would change quickly if whomever it was in that side room were to join the pack. Alexander jerked the barrel of the pistol, anger in his eyes, looking for someone to take his frustration out on. None of us were going to give him the opportunity. We stood at his command. Marcie pushed ahead of me casting a burning stare as she strode past me.

Sherri said, "What is that all about?"

I shrugged. "Why don't you ask her?"

She looked a little startled. "No thank you, darling. I wish to keep my head attached to my shoulders."

Landerfelt lumbered past us and in a single glance managed to accuse me of every foul and evil deed committed in the history of the world. What was he mad about? If I recall, it was he who stuck his nose into my business, not the other way around. If jealousy hadn't got the better of him, he be safe in his wealthy world with all his expensive toys undamaged.

I winced when the pistol punched my spine. "Get moving, Granger." Alexander was being careless. Maybe he'd watched too many cowboy and cop movies? It probably didn't occur to him that getting close enough to a man to prod him with a pistol was a good way to lose the pistol. I supposed with my hands still tied, he felt safe. I figured that was worth a poke in the back and tightened my lips against a smirk; feeling safe was a quick way to end up dead— bound hands or not.

I'd been poked a lot the last several hours and it was getting wearisome. I'd gotten a certain amount of satisfaction working the kid over—call it animal gratification—and I was feeling the urge again. Maybe it was just possible I was beginning to enjoy the sensation, although I wouldn't admit to it in polite company. Sometimes life gets a little stale doing the same things day in and out. For some curious reason that I'm sure psychologists would have a field day investigating, I felt more alive than I had for a good many years. The constant trickle of adrenaline probably had something to do with the feeling, and as soon as that let up, I'd come back to a sound mind and appreciate the humdrum existence as a college biology teacher. Just the same, it had felt good taking Pretty Boy down even if I did end up paying painfully for the pleasure.

Now the animal inside me wanted to turn on the man in the plaid shirt and go for the throat, but good, common sense won out. Even if I could disarm him, Alexander would be a big, brawny wildcat, and probably more than I could handle with bound hands and a head still pounding.

With Sherri grasping my arm, and a hand on the railing to steady myself, I hammed up my weak condition as we made our way down a long flight of steps to the lower level. Sherri bore my extra weight without complaint.

In the mountains you can't simply dig a hole for a basement like you can on flat land. Here you have to engineer a hole using heavy equipment and lots of dynamite. Reaching the lower level and looking around, I decided this hole had cost the owner almost as much as the whole upper portion had and it occurred to me it might have been designed with a secondary purpose in mind. Add an air filtering system, a stash of food, and a deep, protected well for water, and one could hide out down here for a long time—long enough for a cloud of radiation to dissipate?

The place had definitely been decorated by a man. Thinking about it, I hadn't noted anything about the house that would suggest a woman had lent a hand in the decor. The floor was paved in the same tile as the story above, except for a big, red rectangle of carpeting in the center where a pool table resided. A large television was built into one wall. An even larger aquarium, stocked with eating-size fish gliding along a gravel bottom, in and out of big chunks of coral, was built into another wall. A fireplace faced an arrangement of chairs and a sofa, upholstered in saddle leather and polished oak, lending a western flair to the big room. Two wagon wheel chandeliers reinforced the cowboy theme. The wet bar resembled something out of a movie saloon scene, and judging from the bottles behind it, had been stocked by someone who took his drinking seriously.

"Keep on prancing," Alexander said when I paused to run my fingers along the gleaming wood of the pool table. It was a high-class item with six woven leather pockets instead of ramps that roll all the balls to one end of the table. I suspected that if I could peek beneath the sheet of green felt I'd find a slab of real slate, not the cheap particle board you mostly find today. A rack of cues stood at the corner of the red carpeted island. "The table is strictly off limits to you. The amenities are for a different sort of guest than yourself. Don't get your lips set on any libations, either."

"Someone knows how to wine and dine their guests—someone with money and influence?" I didn't expect the question to bring me anything, and it didn't. Alexander's expression remained unreadable and he motioned toward a door.

I said, "I'm not real familiar with this part of Colorado. Was that the town of Breckenridge we flew over just before landing?" Marcie was trying to get my attention, but we couldn't talk here. Maybe I was probing too close to the truth and she was warning me to keep my mouth shut.

"I wouldn't know," he lied.

I shrugged and started moving again. "Good skiing, I hear, Breckenridge." Louis unlocked a door, pushed it open, and ducked inside. A light came on and a moment later the giant stooped out the door and moved to one side as Alexander herded the four of us inside.

Hurried footsteps sounded on the stairs. Raymond came across the room in a quick, long strides and said to Alexander, "Cockran wants to talk to him." He pointed at me.

For some reason that seemed to irritate Alexander, and I wondered again what kind of troubled brewed between him and Cockran. "All right," he said sharply. "You see that they get locked in. I'll take Granger." His scowl shifted toward me. "Come on."

Marcie was still trying to get my attention. I wished she'd settle down before someone noticed. I'd already made the brilliant deduction myself and it really wasn't all that startling.

CHAPTER 16

Wearing frowning lips and brooding eyes, Alexander indicated that I go ahead of him up the stairs. I took my time using the railing to pull myself along just to demonstrate how weak I was.

In the Great Hall he said briefly, "Straight ahead." We crossed the floor to a hallway on the far side. The big door to the outside was unguarded, but he knew I wouldn't attempt to make a dash for it. A .45 caliber pistol pointing at your thoracic vertebrae tends to make you obedient.

The hallway, unlike the Great Room, was carpeted not tiled, and ended a dozen feet or so at a wall with a huge painting that looked as if a drunken monkey had been turned loose in a paint factory. Someone had to be equally drunk to have spent good money buying it, and the jet-black frame, but that's just me who prefers his artwork to represent something recognizable. At least it was somewhat hidden back here. We didn't go as far as the crazy splashes of color but turned into the first door on the left. A second door a few steps farther on was closed.

The room was small, painted flat white, starkly furnished, and carpeted in a coppery colored shag. A large mirror filled one wall behind a gray metal office desk with and a gray metal chair. The desk held an ashtray. The only other furnishings were a burnt orange La-z-Boy chair parked next to a small, round table with a pole lamp sprouting from its middle. There was a small, round grille in the ceiling that might have even played music if the right switch were turned.

Cockran stood next to the desk puffing a cigarette. He'd ditched the suit jacket. Although the temperature here was not warm, perspiration streamed from his forehead and soaked gray crescents into the shirt, under his arms. "Sit down, Granger."

"I'd prefer to stand, if that's okay?"

"As you wish." He crushed the cigarette into the ashtray and lit up another one. "You can leave us," he said to Alexander, flagging a hand toward the door.

I stood there waiting as Alexander left, closing the door behind him. My hands felt as if they had begun to swell a bit from being tied up for a couple hours now. The large mirror, I noted, had been built into the wall, not simply hung on it.

Cockran offered me a cigarette.

"No thank you," I said politely. At this point, a meek demeanor and bowing to his authority was the safest way to proceed.

"Don't smoke?"

"Never developed the habit."

"You're smart," he said in a voice that suggested he'd tried to quit and failed, maybe so many times he'd resigned himself to the addiction.

I said, "You didn't bring me here to discuss my personal habits."

"That observation extends beyond your personal habits, I hope."

His point was clear. I said, "I'd like to think so." I didn't mind the small talk. I was in no hurry for the serious questions to begin.

He studied the coppery carpet for a long, introspective moment and then asked, "What is it you do, Granger?"

"You mean for a living?" I asked just to make sure. He nodded.

"I teach biology at a small southwestern university.

"A college professor?" That seemed to surprise him. "Okay, college professor, what's in this for you?" He'd begun pacing and puffing, and I felt a little like a specimen on display in front of that mirror, a wee beastie under Leeuwenhoek's primitive microscope. Who was in the next room observing us? The answer to that question would have answered a lot of other questions too.

I lifted my bound hands. "Any chance we can get rid of these?"

He stared at them, thinking.

I said, "I'm not going to try anything here, and even if I was foolish enough to think I could overpower you; the cavalry would come riding over the hill in about five seconds." I nodded toward the mirror. "I'd likely be a lot more talkative if I wasn't worrying about my fingers falling off."

Cockran grinned and gave a short laugh. "Funny

guy, huh? I won't need the cavalry to handle a dizzy head like you." He fished a diminutive Swiss Army Knife from his pocket and cut the ropes. "That better?"

I massaged my hands and wrists, blood burning into my fingers. "Thank you. Nothing in the usual sense."

Cockran gave a blank look. "Huh?"

"You asked what was in it for me."

His view narrowed. "Go on."

"You might call it a mild sense of patriotism, or you might call it a way to earn a few extra bucks." The lie came too easily, and it occurred to me that I may have hung around Marcie too long.

"Patriotism!" His harsh retort carried a disgusted note. "Patriotism is for naive young men who believe the propaganda those thugs in Washington tell them. Patriotism is a mental illness that turns good, moral, innocent children into killers. I was in drafted into that war the thugs called a police action to end run Congress. Patriotism? Huh. When the Gooks had me in chains, I made a deal."

"You collaborated with the enemy?" I guess that sounded pretty naive.

His eyes narrowed slightly as he circled me like a wolf on the prowl. "Enemy? Were they my enemy? I didn't know them; they didn't know me. They never harmed me or my family. Why should I want to kill them? It was me who had invaded their country with a gun, they hadn't invaded mine. Hell yes, I collaborated, and I wasn't the only one. I could name names, and one or two of them you'd know. You might call us the Tokyo Roses of Vietnam."

"I guess it's all a matter of point of view. You chose

one side and I the other."

He took a moment to think through what he'd just told me and then put the anger aside. He finished his cigarette, dropping the butt into the ashtray. "You do this often?"

"Occasionally. After the war I completed my Ph.D. in biology and got a job teaching, but Washington doesn't lose track of former employees, especially ones with my talents." If I was going to spread BS, I might as well ladle it on thick. If Cockran and whomever was behind the mirror thought they'd hooked a big fish, they might be less cavalier about the way they reeled him in.

He paced the small room twice, thinking it over. "You'll find me a most intolerant man if you fail to appreciate the seriousness of the moment, Granger."

Muffled footsteps sounded in the hallway outside the door. Farther down the hall the other door opened and closed.

"I do appreciate the seriousness," I assured him.

Impatient fingers dug another cigarette from the wrinkled pack. The lighter clicked, touched fire to it, and snapped shut. "Back on the plane you suggested making a deal."

I gave a short laugh and smiled. "I may have been a naive young man once, Cockran, but those days are long behind me. Soon as I tell you what you want to know...on your terms...you'll drop me in a snowbank somewhere and I won't be found until the spring melt. There's nothing in it for me talking a deal with you, and you know it, but I can offer you one on my terms. Tell me what I want to know and I'll put in a good word for you and not even mention Hanoi Rose." I gripped the chair's arms to keep my hands from shaking. My chest was tight and my heart pounding, but I put on a confident front just like they do in spy movies. "Face it, Cockran. You've blown your cover bringing me here. In a couple hours this place will be swarming with Feds. They'll get you, and you-know-who." I hitched my head toward the one-way mirror.

What did I have to lose? Nothing. But I had everything to gain spinning a story for him. I had no idea what the plot was or how it was all going to end, but if nothing else it might buy me time.

He looked guardedly amused. "A moment ago, you observed correctly that I chose one side of it while you took the other. Like you said, the powers that be don't lose track of their own. As it turns out, your side allows its members to leave the ranks and peruse other ventures. My side does not. We balance upon a very narrow ledge between success and failure and believe me when I tell you that failure is dealt with swiftly and permanently. Should I fail and retribution does not come from your side, it will surely come from mine. So, you see, I have little choice. Now, shall we resume? You can make this easy on yourself or quite difficult."

"I have nothing to tell you," I said, which was one of the few honest statements I'd made to him so far.

"Then we do it the hard way." He hooked a finger at the mirror. Down the hallway a door opened again and then the door to the room opened and Louis ducked under the door frame. Steel fingers crushed my shoulders as the long-boned creature with double the strength of a normal man held me in place while staring at me from beneath hooded eyebrows.

"Don't hurt him...yet."

The vise grip let up slightly.

Cockran loosened his tie, preparing for the hard work ahead. "Let's start over, Granger." He wasn't so big as he was thick and overweight. I wouldn't have had a problem taking him down if not for the giant who stood behind the chair. Louis would definitely be a problem. He had twice my strength and once again my reach. But he moved haltingly, clumsily, and that would work to my advantage if the opportunity presented itself. On the other hand, my head hurt and I was pretty sure I had a concussion. How much of one remained to be seen.

"Tell me what you know about Carl Manquist."

Marcie had not mentioned Carl's last name. I could only hope Cockran was referring to the same Carl. "He learned what you were up to and you killed him to keep him quiet." That was a long-shot answer.

"Who was he working for? His contact?"

I let go of a silent breath. The long shot paid off. "I don't know who he reported to," I said, which I figured was a reasonable enough reply.

He glanced at Louis and gave a small nod. Iron fingers dug beneath my clavicles sending me writhing deep into the chair, fighting back a groan.

"Negative answers will not be tolerated."

Louis let up. I gave a deep moan, straightening and said, "Then I'm in big trouble. We work on a need-to-know. I was brought in as a pinch hitter at the bottom of the ninth. I didn't have a need to know too much."

He didn't buy that. "Marcie wouldn't be as upset with you as she obviously is if you had nothing of value to give us."

"I don't know who Carl reported to. Far as I know he never relayed the info to Marcie. If he did it's just one more thing she failed to tell me. Carl had other contacts that I'm sure you're aware of. Ask one of them." I cast a wary glance to Louis. Cockran's expression remained unreadable. Whether or not he believed me, at least he didn't sic the giant on me again.

"You say they brought you in unprepared. Why would they do that?"

I ignored his sarcasm and said matter-of-factly. "Marcie went missing. I was nearby and available, so they yanked me away from what I was doing, which by the way was a lot more fun than what I'm doing now, and a lot safer. Well, the local trout population might dispute that."

He scowled. "Being flippant will only attract Louis's attention."

Louis showed me a thin line of yellowed teeth.

"I was fishing, honest. I got a call at my brother's cabin—I gambled he didn't know there wasn't telephone service that far out yet—and was told to head up a certain road to a certain spot and keep fishing, but be alert for Marcie, whom they expected to make an appearance. You know the rest of it. It was your hounds that found us.

"Who called you? What's your contact's name?" He leaned close enough for me to smell the tobacco on his breath. "Your contact!" he demanded.

I stared back at him; my mouth stubbornly shut. Two reasons; I didn't want him to think I was being too willing to pass critical information, but more pragmatically, I didn't have a contact or a name to give him. I'd bluffed my way this far but sooner or later he'd see through the ruse.

Cockran signaled Louis and strong fingers plunged beneath my clavicles. This time controlling my reaction was impossible and I gasped a cry of pain and tried to melt into the seat cushions. When Cockran finally waved the giant off I wasn't seeing clearly and my heart was wanting to burst through my chest. My breathing came in gasps, no strength left to even attempt to straighten myself up in the chair. Louis picked me up and got me more or less arranged properly.

Cockran shook the last cigarette from the pack and put it between his lips and casually stated that he'd seen Louis rip men's bones from their chest. My brain was whirling and my vision out of focus. The cigarette bobbed as he spoke, detached from reality, like something out of a cartoon. "It isn't a pretty sight. Now, who is your contact at STE?"

"Go to hell."

I think I read somewhere that this sort of torture had been invented by the Chinese some centuries ago. They had a knack for discovering certain pressure points that generated the most pain without doing permanent damage. Louis must have taken lessons under one of the masters of the technique. Cockran allowed the giant to indulge himself while

I choked on my groans until mercifully uncon-sciousness took away the pain.

A cold splash of water brought me back around and with it the pain too. My shoulders and neck were on fire, not to mention my head still aching from its previous encounter with Alexander's steel pipe. Cockran swam in and out of my vision, gradu-ally sharpening to a fat, smiling Satan. He no longer reminded me of that dentist I used to go to.

He placed a Styrofoam cup on the desk and turned back, looking pleased with himself. "It can get worse, Mr. Granger. Much worse. Shall I have Louis continue?"

It hurt to shake my head. "No...no, that won't be necessary," I groaned.

"Good." The word came out with a puff of gray smoke.

"I said, "Let's talk that deal."

He shook his head. "No deal. That opportunity is past."

"What do I gain by talking?" I asked, my brain scurrying around looking for a back door out of here.

"The satisfaction of seeing Louis walk out the door?"

From behind me came a low, throaty growl that sounded a lot like a character from an old, ghoulish television series. That had been comedy and fantasy. Louis was neither funny nor make believe, and I'd not be sorry to see him leave. I said, "All right. Get rid of Lurch and I'll talk."

The giant swatted me across the back of my head. Cockran nodded toward the door and the one-man torture chamber lumbered out the room.

I said, "Bet he's handy to have around for crushing beer cans and tearing telephone books."

"Louis has his uses."

I tried rotating my arm and winced. The appendage worked after a fashion, but I wasn't going to be casting a line anytime soon, which meant the local trout population had been given a reprieve.

"A name, Mr. Granger, or I will invite Louis back in here."

I'd stalled as long as I could, as long as my battered body wanted to endure Cockran's method of questioning, at least, and blurted the first name that came to mind. "Jacob Marley," I said, immediately wishing I picked someone else. I only hoped he hadn't read Dickens and didn't make the connection.

"Marley?" Cockran's eye lids narrowed. "There's no one at STE by that name."

I gave a silent sigh of relief. He hadn't made the connection. "Marley doesn't work for Space Technologies and Electronics. He's employed by the University; the Agricultural Extension." Recalling my impression of the vegetation planted around the STE facility I saw where this fiction was going and felt more confident as the story came together. "He's a consultant to your maintenance people, advising them on all that fancy greenery growing around your building. He recommends things—you know, fertilizers, how often to use them, how long to water and when, companion species that thrive together and which ones ought to be kept apart, which are shade loving, which like full sunlight. Agronomy can be a challenge here in Colorado, this being a northern extension of the Upper Sonoran Ecoregion." A lot of this information dump was introductory material to a Botany 101 class I taught in at ENMU. I was stalling for time, and also hoping to add credibility to the yarn I was spinning. It gave me a few extra seconds to think ahead to where I was going with all this.

Cockran didn't seem impressed with my horticultural expertise. "How does Marley get access? The grounds people are separate from the engineers."

"He hangs around," I said. "Sometimes has coffee and donuts with the men at break time. I'm guessing he has a contact on the inside, but whomever he or she or they are, I don't know. Like I said, I was pulled into this with little notice and no briefing."

"Marcie was one of those contacts?"

I nodded. "Most likely that's how he knew she'd gone missing."

"Why was she planted on us?"

"STE builds electronics for nuclear warheads. Don't you think certain departments in the government what to keep an eye on that?"

"CIA? FBI?"

I gave a short. "Good luck. It's an agency you've never heard of. Part of military intelligence."

"Hmmm." He frowned and shoved his hands into his pockets, staring a moment at the big mirror behind the desk. I tested the strength in my still-tingling arms. They were pretty useless. He turned sharply, his eyes narrowly focused. "Okay. We can take care of the girl. Back to Manquist. He told Marcie something and she told it to you. Don't say she didn't. Suppose you tell me."

"You know what he told her. Why ask me?"

"I'd prefer to hear it from you." Cockran's false politeness bordered on contempt. He'd pushed me into a corner and the only way out was to tell him what he already knew...something I didn't know. My fingers had started a nervous tarantella on the chair's arm and I willed them to stop as I scrambled to collect my thoughts. "He discovered what you were up to," I said unconvincingly.

"Yes, you've already told me that. You're sweating, Mr. Granger. Is it getting warm in here for you? I'd open a window, but as you can see there aren't any in this room. Just as well. The temperature's been falling since we landed. Near zero last I looked. Too cold to be opening windows. It would be unfortunate for anyone to find themselves outside without a coat."

"No, it's just fine in here," I replied, rotating my arm. I was getting some range back, though the motion hurt. "Your overgrown sidekick did a job on my arm."

"What a shame." His voice hardened. "Manquist. What did he tell Marcie?"

"If I don't tell you you're going to sic your pet person on me again?"

He raised an arm toward the mirror and then suddenly switched motion and swung across with the back of his hand. My teeth ground together and I tumbled from the chair. I looked up at him from the floor, standing over me, clenched fists and anger flaring in his eyes.

"Anything that needs doing here I can take care of myself. I've just learned something, Granger. You have no idea what Manquist discovered, and if you don't, odds are neither does the girl." He'd lost the cigarette from his mouth and his shoe came down and ground it out on the carpet. Reaching for the pack in his pocket and discovering it empty, he cursed and cast it savagely aside, signaling the mirror. A moment later Louis bent beneath the door frame.

"Take him out of here then have the speeder brought up from the hangar."

A big hand grabbed the back of my neck, lifted me to my feet and shoved me toward the door.

"You're making a mistake." Words of a desperation said over my shoulder, but not completely lacking truth. I'd managed to figure a few things out in the short time we'd been in the house; little clues had triggered something I recalled seeing on TV, or maybe I'd read it in the local newspaper. Being a New Mexican, I'd not paid much attention to local Colorado politics, but that didn't mean I hadn't pick up odd bits of it here and there. It's what Marcie had been trying to warn me about, but I'd already figured it out myself. I grabbed the door jamb to break my forward momentum and turned back toward Cockran, looking past him at the big mirror. "What will this do to Senator Stratterford's chances of reelection once our people break the story to the newspapers."

Louis came to a halt, his brooding eyes widening.

Cockran went rigid looking at me, not speaking. For an instant time seemed to have entered a holding pattern. Then the overhead speaker crackled, a man's voice filled the room.

"Sten, I want to talk with you. Bring Mr. Granger back into the room. Louis can watch him."

Scowling, Cockran avoided my eyes as he strode out into the hallway, loudly shutting the door behind him. Louis made himself a human barricade in front of it as I sat back in the chair. It had been a guess, a real long shot this time. It felt pretty good to be right for a change. I grinned up at Louis. His face remained as emotionless, immovable, like one of those stone heads in South Dakota.

CHAPTER 17

The senator from Colorado was not a young man. He looked older now than the sixty-five-or-so I'd have guessed his true age to be. Worry does that to a body, and judging from the pinched expression he wore now, worrying is what he'd been doing. Even so, middle age had treated him kindly. Lester Stratterford had managed to dodge the practically unavoidable midriff spread that comes to most folks watching summer recede in the rearview mirror and the fall years quickly approaching ahead. Judging from his nut-brown skin he'd spent a lot of time out of doors, but I had a feeling the bleached-blond hair had been helped along with a bottle of Lady Clairol—or whatever brand hair dye it was men used these days.

He presented an impressive image of robust health that appealed to the younger constituency that Marcie suggested he tried to woo. What was it she'd called him? A peacenik...and maybe a few other terms not near as flattering.

He'd been frowning when Louis had escorted me into the room behind the mirror and now, with dipped eyebrows, he studied me from behind a wide, oak desk. Cockran stood at one corner of it. A large window with its view to the fluorescent-lit room I'd just left stood brightly contrasted to the subdued warm hues of this place. A wall of floor to ceiling windows showed a snowy, forested mountainside. Bookcases made of some dark wood hugged two walls and oak paneling covered what remained. The room smelled of oiled wood, leather, and pipe tobacco. On a corner of the desk was a silver tray with a crystal decanter containing a golden liquid. Two huge, potted philodendrons stood in front of the tall windows, and a pair of guards hovered quietly in the background. In the daylight the office would be bright and warm; a pleasant place to work or receive important visitors.

Louis brought me to a halt in front of the desk. Senator Stratterford peered at me through contemplated eyes as a doctor might a patient in whom he'd just diagnosed a rare and fatal disease. After a few moments he said, "How did you know?"

I said, "You're a well-known man, Senator." I didn't mention that I'd only been vaguely aware of his existence up until a day ago.

"Indeed. I am a public figure, however, certain aspects of my life I wish to keep private."

"Doesn't that become problematic when you shine a spotlight on yourself by supporting protest marches on government contractors and openly embracing communism, especially with the growing tensions between the US and the USSR?" I'd gleaned this much by what little Marcie had told me about Stratterford.

He looked amused. "You twist my stance on the issues, Mr. Granger."

"I do?"

He stopped smiling. "Answer the question."

"One of Alexander's men mentioned your name at the cabin where Marcie was being held, and she told me." I glance around the room. "This is an expensive house located in a major ski resort. Your reputation for being an outdoorsy type precedes you. I wasn't certain at first, of course, but I suspected all this belonged to you, sir."

"Your instincts are good, Mr. Granger." He leaned back in his chair. "Earlier you said the Feds will be arriving. How would you know this, and how would they know where we are?"

He appeared to be buying my explanation, or at least not immediately discounting it. "That's easy. I had a backup man. He followed us to the airport. It's certain he took note of the tail numbers on your plane and traced it back to its owner...you, sir."

He looked startled, and then the tension left his face and I knew my last remark had been a mistake. "Good, very good." He took a sip of his brandy and said, "All the loose ends neatly tied up in a fancy, well thought out ribbon...I don't believe a word of it. It's too clean. Even if true, the aircraft is registered to the STE Corporation." He laughed and waved a hand. "Take him away, Louis. Sten, you may proceed arranging for a dreadful accident."

I said, "If I'm going to die for something, can I at least know what it is?"

"You really don't?" Stratterford asked.

I shrugged and turned my palms to the ceiling. There was nothing to be gained carrying on the ruse any longer. The game was over. From here on out I had only one objective, and that was staying alive. The odds of that weren't looking too good at the moment. "Truth is, I'm here because I was in the wrong place at the wrong time when Marcie Rose stumbled into my life."

Stratterford glanced at Cockran who was fidgeting with the lighter in his pocket, looking desperately in need of a cigarette. Apparently, the Senator didn't keep any around. Well, cigarettes wouldn't exactly fit the man's public image of robust health, I guess. "It's been a bluff, Sten."

Cockran said defensively, "He knew about Carl. He knew about you."

"He was guessing. He tossed us a few crumbs that he'd picked up from the girl and filled in the blanks with guesswork." He looked back at me. "Isn't that right, Mr. Granger."

"You figured it out, sir. That's why you're the Senator and Sten here is hired help." It never hurt to stroke the ego of the man in control.

Stratterford laughed. "We've been had, Sten."

Cockran didn't see the humor. "I'll get rid of him," he said and moved toward me.

"Not so fast. A resourceful fellow like Mr. Granger would appreciate what we've been doing under the snooping noses of all those *alleged* agents working at STE. It will give him something to think about while slowly shivering to sleep."

"I don't think..." Between the two of them, Cockran plainly had the street smarts.

"I do the thinking around here, Sten."

Biting back his reply, Cockran locked eyes with the Senator a moment and then glanced away. Cockran might have street smarts, but he knew who cracked the whip. "I'll have Raymond bring up the speeder. I'll feel easier about this once the four of them are out of the way."

Stratterford spoke more gently. "Everything will work out fine. You'll see."

"I hope so." He didn't sound convinced, and left the room, closing the door behind him.

"Sten's a good man, but he's problem oriented not solution," Stratterford poured a small amount of brandy into a snifter and brought it over to me. He was about my height and our eyes met even. "I intend to have you killed, Mr. Granger, but I see no reason to be uncivilized about it. Nothing personal, you understand." He handed me the snifter.

"Sure. I understand. That doesn't make the prospect of dying any less horrifying." I tasted the brandy. It burned all the way down to the middle of my empty stomach.

"You really didn't know what's been going on, did you."

"Not a blessed thing, sorry to say."

He smiled and shook his head. "You had my men in a something of a panic, you and the girl."

"But not you?"

"I had concerns. That's why you and your friends are here."

"And now you're convinced?" I took another sip. It didn't burn quite so much as the first.

"About you? More or less."

"But not Marcie Rose?"

"From what I'm told Matthew's secretary was a bit too nosy, a bit too confident. I'm certain she's not what she claims to be, and that her disappearance will likely make a few official waves, but not enough to scuttle our boat, I think."

"She probably had secretarial training, among her many other talents. Personally, I haven't been able to figure out exactly what she is, except, of course, a consummate liar."

Stratterford seemed to appreciate my summation of Marcie Rose. "What about the others?" he asked.

"Sherri Lane. She's a friend, and the daughter of a very rich and powerful family who've lived in Colorado Springs for several generations. Her father has money... enough to find out what happened to his daughter should she turn up missing. Ditto for the chubby fellow, Brian Landerfelt. He and Sherri grew up together among the well-heeled of the Broadmoor neighborhood. Sherri is a sort of champion of the poor and underprivileged. Brian didn't qualify in that regard. I on the other hand was eminently qualified. Both of them are completely innocent of whatever it is Marcie is involve in, and both come from families that can make big trouble if you harm them."

"More trouble if allowed to leave here, especially if the girl is a crusader as you claim she is."

There was no arguing that. I said, "Since it can't matter too much now, I'm curious why it is you're involved in this? I mean, a United States Senator is a plush job. Why risk it?"

"Yes," he considered a moment, "it can't matter now." There was a finality in his tone that drove home the stark reality of the situation the four of us were in. "Like your friend, Miss Lane, I have my own cause that I champion." He paused considering how to continue. "I don't know how, but Manquist discovered that someone was exchanging high quality components for faulty one in the assembly of the RD 35 Detonator package. The swapped units had been manufactured in a nation that is...well, shall we say not on friendly terms with the west."

"It's not hard to guess which one that might be."

Stratterford smiled thinly. "The units are brought in by way of diplomatic pouch. They function flawlessly for a specified time and then burn out, rendering the detonators inoperative."

I said, "A warhead containing such a detonator would slam harmlessly into its target."

"He nodded. "That is the general idea."

"Alexander, being head of quality control, passed them through the system and no one was the wiser... until Carl Manquist discovered what was happening."

"How did he figure it out?" I knew what Marcie had told me. I wondered how far his people had gotten on the problem.

"We are in the process of learning how that happened and rectifying the matter."

"By *rectifying the matter,* you mean the elimination Carl Manquist and the four of us?"

"Unfortunate, but it is necessary." He sounded sincere. "Anything else, Mr. Granger?"

A gift of a few sips of brandy and a couple moments of civilized talk—well, he'd done his best to prove to me and to himself that he wasn't a heartless murderer, and now with a clean conscience he was free to get rid of me...us. "Just one more thing."

"Yes?"

"Marcie said you intend to replace the entire US arsenal with these new detonators. Is that true?"

"Yes."

"That's quite clever. Disarm the country without removing its weapons."

"You disapprove?"

"The plan has a certain charm, if you think the USSR blowing the US off the map is charming."

"Tsk-tsk-tsk. We shouldn't mention names. Your deduction has a flaw in it."

"That is?" I asked.

"What good is a radioactive chunk of real estate to anyone?"

"Ah, I think I understand. Not war, but ransom?"

"War is so messy," Stratterford said, "and unnecessary. "New York City should suffice. If the message goes unheeded, then maybe Los Angeles will make our intentions clear. I doubt we'll have to go so far as to incinerate Washington, DC. The simple fact is, Americans haven't the stomach for a real war, nor the ability to win one. Vietnam proved that."

I was aware of Louis standing behind me like a giant attack dog waiting for his master's command.

I said, "I don't suppose it will do any good to say you won't get away with it?"

He gave a short laugh and said, "I was expecting something more original. Clichés don't become you Mr. Granger." He removed the glass from my fingers and nodded at Louis. "Goodbye, Mr. Granger."

Louis's baseball mitt covered my shoulder and turned me toward the door.

CHAPTER 18

"Paul!" Sherri rushed to where I'd landed and took my hand. With her assistance I got myself up off the floor in time to see Louis back out of the room and close the door.

"Are you all right, Paul?"

My shoulders screamed, my arms were rubber, and my head pounded. Any halfway competent doctor would have ordered me to bed for a week. I didn't know what kind of damage being bounced about by a fellow like Louis would do to a brain suffering from a concussion, but I was pretty sure no good could come from it. "I'm okay," I lied as she helped me to a chair and helped me ease into it.

The room was moderately sized, comfortably furnished, a coppery carpet giving it a warm, cozy feeling. A row of windows near the ceiling was the only indication that we were in a basement. Brian, bent forward in a chair in the corner, had stopped dabbing his split lip with a handkerchief when Louis had cast me across the room. Brian watched Sherri and me a

moment, then turned his gloomy view away and re-
sumed pressing the bloodied handkerchief to his lips.

Marcie stood against the wall near a table, left
arm folded across her stomach, right hand bringing a cigarette to her lips. She'd managed to bum a
smoke off of someone and was hungrily inhaling the
nicotine. Like Cockran, she was hooked. She pushed
away from the wall and came over to us.

"They work you over?" she asked matter-of-factly.

"Not too bad," I said not much in a mood to relate
the details of Louis's exploits of the last half hour.

"What did you tell them?"

"The truth," I said bringing a finger to my lips and
pointing at the speaker grille overhead. She was still
supposed to be angry with me and she grasped the
situation without any further coaching.

"So you told them everything about you, about
them, about me?" Marcie said loudly, and then whispered, *"What's the setup?"*

"Already told you that, Miss. Rose, I explained
that Sherri, Brian and me, we're victims of the
wrong place and wrong time syndrome. It didn't
make any difference to Senator Stratterford," then
quietly added, *"They're taking us out of here in
something called a speeder, to arrange an accident."*

"Stratterford? You mean that wacko peacenik
is involved in this?" she nearly shouted with mock
surprise in her voice. *No one will discover our
bodies full of bullet holes then,"* she whispered
matter-of-factly.

"I guess we shouldn't be surprise considering
who his friends on the left are. *Bullet holes make*

for unconvincing accidents."

Marcie said, "You've turned out to be one hell of a partner. *We'll need to make our move now or it's never."*

"Cut the crap, Marcie. I told Stratterford everything, remember? Anyway, I never asked to be a part of this, if you recall. This is what I...we...get for trying to help you out of a tight spot. *Our best chance is some kind of diversion while they're taking us out of here."*

Sherri, suddenly suspicious, came over and said, "What are you two doin-"

I clamped a hand over her mouth and put my lips close to her ear. A delicious remnant of perfume clung to her messed hair. "The room is bugged. Careful what you say."

She stared at me a startled, wide-eyed moment, then the light of understanding snapped on. "You're making plans?" she whispered, glancing at Marcie.

I nodded.

"What can I do to help?"

Brian was watching us from the chair in the corner, giving me a look that made me uneasy. More trouble on the wind, I worried, coming from his direction. To Sherri I said, *"When the time comes bite and scratch and kick like hell."*

"How will I know when it's time?"

"You'll know because I'll be biting and scratching and kicking like hell too." Then in an angry voice I barked, "This is between Marcie and me. Stay out of it." If someone was actually listening in on us, I didn't want them to think all was chummy here. Let

them waste time wondering.

Brian slid off his chair and said, "Don't talk to Sherri that way."

I was right. The trouble wind had begun to blow. The big boy was angry. Maybe there was some hope after all. "I'll talk to her any way I want to." Anger was good, I decided. When Stratterford's goons came for us, the more anger the better.

Sherri went to him and took his arm. "It okay, Brian," she said.

He freed himself from her grasp in a reckless show of bravado. "It's not all right for him to talk to you like you were a nobody."

"Brian! Just stay out of it."

For a moment I thought he'd become a changed man, but I was mistaken. His head dropped to his chest and the determination in his voice drained away. "We can't just sit here doing nothing."

I said, "We're open to suggestions."

"We can try to break down the door," he said with a catch in his voice.

"It's made of steel," I said mildly.

"We can at least try."

I offered him the door. "Give it your best shot, Mr. Landerfelt. Once you burst through it, assuming you can, what do you propose to do with the armed guard that's likely standing on the other side?"

His voice rose an octave. "But we can't just sit here waiting for them to return and...and shoot us... or something."

In spite of having lived a largely sheltered life, Brian Landerfelt had a realistic grasp of the situation facing us. "I don't see as we have much choice at the moment," I said for the benefit of any ears that might be listening in on the drama playing out here.

He gave me a disbelieving look. "You're being awful calm about all this, Granger."

Marcie laughed. "It's just his easygoing nature," she said mockingly. "Don't let it fool you, Landerfelt, Granger is this close to shitting his pants full."

Sherri gave her a disapproving look.

Marcie turned on her. "Don't get all high and mighty little Miss Prissy. Maybe if you got off that marble tower and played in the dirt a while, you'd be able to hold onto your man."

Sherri's face showed a viciousness I'd never expected to see there. "Why you little hussy!" Fist clenched she went for Marcie.

I caught her wrist just in time. "You don't want to tangle with her, Sherri," I said soothingly.

"You heard what she said."

"Believe me, you don't want to mix it up with her."

Marcie laughed. "Afraid I'll break your china doll, Granger?" She put her hands on her hips and stood there, a grin on her face. "The three of you deserve each other."

Sherri looked wildly at me. I said softly, "Hold that feeling for when it's needed."

She glared hotly, and then the fire cooled and she glanced up at the ceiling grille. *"This is all part of some plan, isn't it, Paul?"*

I nodded. *"We're all one big unhappy family here. Understand?"* Her expression told me we were all on the same page now. She took Landerfelt by the arm and tugged the big, reluctant fellow off to one side and spoke quietly into his ear. I don't know what she said, but afterwards the anger had left him too.

Marcie had smoked her cigarette down to the filter and jabbed it into an ashtray on one of the tables. Sherri remained near Brian while I watched the door. There was some noise on the other side of it. Muffled voices came through the steel panel. I took a couple deep breaths, getting ready. After a little while a lock clicked and Alexander, Raymond, and Louis came in.

I noted only the one pistol among them, the .45, but I hadn't forgotten the pip-squeak .25 in Raymond's pocket. They weren't heavy in the firearms department, but then with Louis there, they probably didn't think bringing in an arsenal was necessary."

"Time to take a ride," Alexander said jerking the pistol at the door. We gathered up our coats, Marcie moving like a spring wound tighter than a mousetrap. My heart felt like a pile driver trying to burst my chest, my breathing coming in short, harsh gasps. I shrugged into my coat and wiped sweat from my forehead. They herded us together outside the door, Raymond taking the lead with Alexander riding drag and Louis following off to one side.

We were passing the pool table when Marcie made her move. She stopped abruptly, glared at me and said, "I'd rather walk beside a skunk than that SOB."

"You're the fucking skunk, bitch, not Paul," sweet, always-proper Sherri snarled. I winced at her back-alley language. Her tongue must be burning, I mused, but the attack had been the perfect catalyst to get things moving in the right direction.

Marcie swung around and glared at her. "Bitch? I can do without anymore of little Miss Prissy's whining."

"Oh, shut up." It wasn't as shocking a retort as Sherri's had been but coming from Brian I figured it was a step in the right direction.

Marcie looked at him, genuine surprise on her face. "So, we finally hear from the Goodyear blimp."

Brian was hefty but *blimp* wasn't exactly an accurate description. It was a cruel but effective jab. Sherri silently watched Marcie deride Brian, and although Sherri understood Marcie's purpose, I saw that she hated her for it.

Raymond gave Alexander a concerned look. Alexander might have been enjoying the exchange; it was hard to read his expression because there wasn't any.

I hadn't expected the whole crew to get in on the charade, but it did make it more convincing, and I suspected it was a well needed emotional release for all of us. I said to Marcie, "Get off his back. This is between you and me."

She wheeled and slapped me hard enough to make my eyes sting; probably leave finger marks on my cheek. Anything less violent would have been suspect and I'm glad it was Marcie doing the slapping and not Sherri who would have held back, not wanting to hurt me too much because, well, that's just Sherri.

I snatched her wrist and wrenched her arm around behind her—she let me do this because if she didn't want it to happen it never would have. Sherri and Brian moved aside scattering Alexander neat grouping. Alexander ordered us to break it up.

I pretended not to hear him, struggling to contain a kicking, bucking Marcie Rose in my arms. Alexander moved closer raising the pistol. Calculating he'd come close enough, I let go of the lady tornado and the gates of hell opened up right there in Senator Stratterford's basement.

A foot rocketed out and the pistol sailed from his hand and bounced off a wall. A look of surprise didn't have time to come to his face before the female polecat was all over him. I figured Alexander was history and put him out of mind, crouching and spinning about to face Raymond and Louis.

Raymond was grappling in his pocket for the tiny gun. My fingers found the only object available, which happened to be a blue, ivory billiard ball in the middle of a sea of green. I'd seen enough baseball to know what a sizzling fast ball looked like, and it's amazing what a big shot of adrenaline will do for one's aim. The sizzler went right down the middle of home plate and Raymond went down hard, spitting up blood. Strike one. The ump called him *out!* A dentist was going to make a bundle of money off him.

A huge shadow moved over me from the left. I leaped aside as a pair of tree limbs came down. With both fists clenched together, I swung into the small of Louis's back. It had the resiliency of a bag of wet sand. The giant stumbled a half step, caught himself on the edge of the pool table. He recovered amazingly fast for a man his size and came at me like an animated forklift. The stretch of his arms fenced me in forcing me back against the long, cool glass of the built-in fish tank; wide shoulders obscuring the light from the big wagon wheel chandelier over the pool table. I zeroed in on the most vulnerable target, snapped up the toe of my boot, and missed. The clumsy maneuver toppled me onto the carpet. Staring up, Chicken Little must have felt a little like this as Louis's bulk obscured the ceiling, big excavator buckets reaching down.

CRACK!

Louis arched backwards as half a cue stick flew past me. The other half, the narrow half, remained in Sherri's white-knuckle grasp. A look of shock stretched her pretty face, realizing what she'd done and surprised at the results. I scurried out between Louis's widespread legs. He shook the fogginess from his brain and staggered to keep his balance. I leaped atop the pool table, pulled back on the chandelier and sailed out feet first driving my weight into the center of his chest. Momentum impelled him backwards and his thick skull crashed through the plate glass aquarium and torrents of water and flopping fish poured from the shattered hole around his neck.

The chandelier brought me back to the table and I jumped off, my feet sloshing onto the wet carpet. Marcie was reaching for something behind a chair. Alexander lay curled on the floor gurgling foamy blood and having a hard time breathing. Brian's wide, startled face stared from the other side of the room where he'd backed up against the cowboy saloon bar. Sherri, still clutched the broken cue stick as if it were made of gold, wore wide eyes too. Not so much frightened or terrified like her ex-boyfriend, they appeared more stunned at the carnage that had occurred in what might have been all of a minute if that long. It hadn't been so long that reinforcements had arrived, but that would be changing soon.

"Thanks," I told her.

She blinked and swallowed a couple times and gave a single nod. Shock had strangled the words in her throat.

Marcie straightened holding the .45. That pistol was making the rounds, I mused. In a glance she took in the massacre, a flicker of a smile reaching her lips when she spied Louis, weakly trying to extradite himself from the shattered tank, tinting the water a pale pink color in the process.

Raymond groaned from the floor, blood dripping through fingers cupped over his mouth. I found the .25 automatic in his pocket and pulled back the slide a quarter inch to check the chamber for a glint of brass. It was loaded.

"Nice going, amigo," Marcie said.

I grimaced. "You'd think I'd get used to mayhem, hanging around you. Now I know why they name hurricanes after women."

"*Women?* Isn't it about time you got off that deserted island you're living on, Granger? They put a stop to that sexist system years ago."

I hadn't been living on an island, and it had only been three years since NOAA began incorporating male names into the hurricane roster, but now wasn't the time to be having this discussion.

Marcie plowed ahead without a pause, "Okay, a plan?" She was talking fast. Like me, she expected the cavalry to come charging down the stair steps at any moment.

I shrugged. "I suppose we ought to be getting out of here."

Her eyes widened with mocking amazement. "Brilliant, Einstein. Can you fly a plane?"

"No."

"I can—after a fashion."

"Then the plan is to make it out to the runway without getting shot full of holes," I replied watching the stairs and listening for the sound of pounding feet. So far so good.

"And that's a very good plan." Marcie started for the staircase.

"But!" Sherri had finally found her voice. She looked at Louis and then to me. "We can't just leave him there to drown."

Marcie's jaw unhinged. "Your prissy girlfriend wants to stay here and nursemaid the beast?"

I gave Marcie a sharp glance. "You can lighten up on the heavy-handed routine now." Caring for people was what Sherri was about and I didn't like it being rubbed in her face. I turned to her and said patiently but firmly, "Sherri, if we don't get out of here now, we never will. We'll be killed and that's certain."

"We can't just leave..."

I took her hand and pulled her after me. She resisted, of course, but I suspected that was only to make it easier on her conscience later on when she thought back on this moment if she...we were lucky enough to live that long.

Marcie took the lead up the stairs. Brian and

Sherri followed. Brian, thank goodness, showed no great compulsion to linger and help the fallen. He seemed quite happy leaving them lay where they'd fallen. Sensible fellow, Brian. My opinion of him hitched up a notch.

At the top of the stairs Marcie peeked around the corner. The whirr of a mildly muffled engine came from somewhere outside the house. The sound of it might have masked the crash and clash of the battle we'd just fought below. Luck had paid us a visit, I mused, knowing that Luck was a fickle lady and might move on at any moment.

"All clear." Marcie glanced bright-eyed back at me, that big .45 in her small hand, my big hand clutching the tiny .25. There seemed an almost comical inconsistency here. I'll admit to being just as brilliantly egotistical as any male, and maybe borderline chauvinistic too, but this was not the time or place to let pride trip us up. Marcie was the more competent of the two of us. She'd make better use of the fire power than I. Besides, for what I knew had to be done, the quiet little .25 was eminently more practical. "What's that sound," she asked.

The low, raspy hum reminded me of a little VW beetle a college girlfriend used to drive. "Sounds like an air-cooled Volkswagen all revved up."

She frowned.

I said, "You ever hear of something called a speeder?"

"No."

"I think I spied one earlier when we got off the plane."

Her forehead furrowed, remembering. "That

funny looking red bathtub parked alongside the hangar?"

"Uh-huh. My guess is it's fitted with a VW engine, a propeller, and a pair of skis."

"Hm. That may be more convenient than the plane. Let's see if your guess is right, Granger." We moved along the hallway single file. It opened onto the great hall. Across the way a pair of men wearing heavy, white parkas were just crossing the wide floor to a door on the other side, their attention ahead, not behind.

When they'd gone, I said, "Doesn't look like anyone called out the cavalry." I glanced toward the closed door the two men had entered. "That means Stratterford hadn't been listening in on the intercom."

Marcie looked worriedly back the way we'd come. "You thinking what I'm thinking, Granger?"

I nodded. "We left three living bodies downstairs and all any one of them has to do is push a call button and everyone on Stratterford's payroll will come charging in." I though a moment, considering the notion I'd had a few minutes earlier, glancing at the diminutive pistol in my hand. "I'll buy us some time. Take Brian and Sherri out of here and get to the plane or the speeder, or even that old jeep by the hangar. I'll take care of the problems in the basement.

"Damn." Marcie grimaced. "I don't like us splitting up now."

"No other way," I said, "now get moving."

"Don't get yourself killed, Granger. I still need you."

I grinned. "Already told you I didn't know how to fly an airplane." I knew that wasn't what she'd meant.

Our relationship had subtly turned a corner. We'd bonded in an unfathomable way that oftentimes happens on a battlefield. She didn't have to say the words. Her eyes showed me what she was feeling.

"Oh, shut up," she said because it was the appropriate thing to say at the moment, and because Marcie wouldn't know how to express a truly tender sentiment. She thrust the .45 at me. "Take it."

"No, you'll need it more than me. You've three people to think about. Besides this peashooter is sufficient for what needs to be done."

Sherri's eyes got big. "Paul, what are you doing. Don't leave."

I didn't what to explain it to her, instead said, "You and Brian go with Marcie. I'll meet up with you in a few minutes."

"But..." she glanced at the pistol and then looked away. She understood.

"Marcie, if there's any trouble-"

"I'll take care of it," she said confidently." Marcie herded them across the foyer to the tall door. A blast of snow swirled inside, the sound of the idling VW engine increased briefly and then subsided as the door closed. I stood there, alone now. We'd need maybe ten more minutes. I was guessing. I didn't know what Marcie was going to encounter out there.

I started back down the staircase. This was something I should have taken care of before we'd left, but I didn't want Sherri or Brian to have to watch. The thought stopped me halfway down the stairs and I stared at the tiny pistol. How long had it been? Ten... twelve...fifteen years? Oddly, I couldn't remember.

Maybe it was the concussion making me forget? That war was over. My job in it over. The files on one Paul Granger closed, and with them all rights and privileges canceled. I was a peaceful, law abiding citizen now. A biology professor at a small-town university who suffered pangs of guilt sacrificing a laboratory rabbit or pithing a frog. And here I was on my way to dispatch three humans to clear a path to freedom and not a single pang of guilt in sight. The white plaster walls about me might just as well have been bamboo; this house in the middle of a steaming jungle instead of on a snowy mountainside above a Colorado ski resort.

Reality is a hard thing to hold onto when the past and present merge. I knew that same surge of excitement, that same twisting terror in my stomach. I thought it had been buried back there in Nam. Resurrected now, the frightening truth was that I was enjoying the feelings.

My reminiscing lasted maybe all of three seconds before I looked away from the gun and returned my thoughts to the task at hand. I could damn well worry about my inner conflicts and murky motivations later. I started down the stairs again with a firm resolve to dispatch Alexander, Louis, and Raymond; to do it quickly and to get out as fast as I can.

I emerged into the basement instinctively knowing something was not right. Before I figured it out, something like a baseball bat slammed down on my wrist and the gun flew from my fist. At the corner of my eye I spied a second bat swinging toward my face.

CHAPTER 19

They weren't Louisville Sluggers; of course, they were Louis sluggers. The first blow landed like a lump of gnarled old hickory at the end of a three-foot shaft. Louis had struck violently as if he was angry at me or something...I guess he had good reasons. At least a dozen cuts and gashes trickled red from his unlovely head and neck like some gruesome character out of some late-night horror movie. The giant was wet, bleeding, and half drowned, and by the wild look in his eyes, he was determined that his right fist was going to grind my nose to mush.

I had other ideas, and just enough time to relocate my face from his incoming trajectory. His fist went through the wall plaster. I tumbled under his arm and hit the carpet in a somersault that brought me back to my feet.

Louis yanked his fist from the wall tearing out a chunk of plasterboard. He shook it off and came toward me in a jerky, mechanical fashion, like a Disney animatronics robot.

I shucked off my coat to give me a bit of freedom to move. He was sluggish due to his medical condition and no doubt his recent encounter with a cue stick and a sheet of aquarium glass, even so, if he managed to get a hand on me, I'd not be rejoining Marcie and the others.

I dodged and half tripped over Alexander's sprawled legs. Regaining my balance, I spied the broken cue stick that had been Sherri's solution to the Louis problem. Unfortunately, it was out of reach. The other sticks were neatly arranged in a rack, also out of reach. The little Colt Junior had disappeared somewhere on the soaked carpet. I retreated from Louis's advance. The stairs were wide open for a quick dash and safe retreat, but that wouldn't solve the problem and the reason I'd come back here.

Hurrying around the corner of the pool table, my foot came down on something slippery and wiggling, and I landed hard on my back. Before I could move and get my breath back, mitt-sized hands caught my shoulders and tossed me like a sack of potatoes against the wall, rattling the broken glass in the aquarium's stainless-steel frame. The hard landing didn't do my concussed brain any good, or my vision. The chandelier over Louis's left shoulder made slow circles of kaleidoscope flashes and the giant had acquired an out-of-focus twin.

I felt myself being lifted from the floor again. Past the carnival flashes, Louis's ugly lips took on a grotesque grin. I kicked, my efforts mostly spent flailing empty air, my strength giving out. It seemed Lady Luck was leaving the room. Well, I knew she was a fickle consort, but as she left, she glanced over her shoulder one last time and blew me a parting kiss. My toe struck Louis where striking a man produces the most pain; not a solid kick, or even one properly placed, but good enough to buckle him at the waist and for his hands to reach instinctively to protect the vital spot.

My shoulder hit the floor; black swirls pulsed before my eyes. Somehow, in spite of all this, I spied the large wedge of aquarium glass laying at my fingertips, a rainbow of light glinting off its smooth surface. I reached for it and missed. My depth perception was way off. I reached again, grabbing up the sharp edge as Louis, in a blind rage swung a fist the size of a watermelon. I moved my head catching his glancing blow, then lunged at his throat.

A spurt of blood hit my chest, and then another. Louis eyes bulged, his hands going instinctively to his neck, crimson fountains forcing their way through clenched fingers in little, rhythmic spurts. He staggered against the pool table, green felt turning red, flopping like a beached shark, dying.

I watched the horror show slowly becoming aware of a fire growing in my hand and the warm flow of blood running down my wrist and arm. I opened my hand, but the large shard of glass just hung there, firmly imbedded in the fleshy web between my thumb and finger.

My attention divided between my own blood and the Louis's blood, dripping into a right corner pocket and pooling upon the carpet beneath it. His wild thrashing slowed to small quivers as his body drained.

I felt sick. I recalled a little Vietnamese soldier who hadn't been much older than fifteen or sixteen, a kid who'd never hurt me or anyone I cared about, dying a similar death. I tried to shake the memory, but hauntings never leave you alone...not completely.

Louis was a big man and a big heart doing its damnedest to empty his huge body of blood. I turned my attention to more immediate concerns. I squeezed my wrist, pretty certain I'd severed the distal loop of the Radial Artery, which was most prominent at the wrist and a favorite target of would-be suicides. In a giddy moment that must have been the onset of shock I recalled in exquisite detail diagramming the Radial Artery on a chalk board for a physiology class I taught each semester. It wasn't a large artery by the time it reached down into the hand, but big enough to bleed a man to death if the flow wasn't stopped.

Raymond watched all this from the floor where he lay with a hand covering his bleeding mouth, his eyes stretched beyond belief at what he'd witnessed. I paused briefly over him as I was leaving, debating cutting his throat too, but there'd been just too damned much blood spilled. I was sick to my stomach of it, of the memories. Raymond was out of the action and not going anywhere. I climbed the stairs, turned into the hallway, and stopped.

"There he is," Cockran shouted to someone just around the corner. The reinforcements had finally arrived. They were plainly searching for someone—for me. That meant something must have gone terribly wrong with Marcie's getaway. I wheeled and headed the other direction leaving a trail of blood. The hallway ended at a pair of glass doors, steam-fogged so that I couldn't see beyond them. I didn't have time to worry about that and pushed through into a room filled with moist, warm air. An intricate pattern of blue and green tiles encompassing a rectangular swimming pool spread out toward a wall of windows. Potted plants and lawn furniture gave the place a tropical feeling here on the snowy slopes of the Rocky Mountains. It all seemed very much out of place against the whiteness of the landscape beyond the steamed windows.

Cockran paused outside the automatic doors and cautiously pushed them open. I pressed against the wall, half hidden behind a heavy redwood patio chair and a small glass table. He advanced cautiously, a revolver extended in front of him, the moist air muffling his footsteps. He was alone and I wondered what had happened to the person he'd spoken too? Cockran glanced toward the water, smooth as blue glass, then slowly moved his view around the natatorium. I was briefly aware of the revving Volkswagen engine before the automatic doors whispered shut.

Before his view found me, I scooped up the little table and flung it at him. My aim had been pretty good in spite of my bleeding hand and woozy brain. It careened off his arm skittering the gun across the floor, and then sailed on a few feet and crashed through one of the tall windows. A cold wind swirled in bringing a flurry of snow with it. Cockran fanned his hand and turned a snarl toward me.

"You don't think you're going to make it out of here?" he said rubbing his right arm. Well, he had to say that just like I had said something similar to Stratterford. They were just words and we both knew it. I was getting worried about the second gent who'd not yet made an appearance, pretty sure he'd show up shortly with reinforcements.

"Spare me the movie dialogue, Cockran," I said scanning the floor for the revolver. It lay against the wall beneath the broken window, too far for any hope of reaching it. "Of course, I intend to get out of here, or at least make sure you don't either." I moved slowly toward the source of the cold wind.

"What happened to the others downstairs?"

"Worried about your pals?" I said sarcastically.

He grinned. "Good help is hard to come by."

I gave a short laugh. "The two short ones were still alive when I left them."

His eyebrows rose. "You killed Louis? I've underestimated you, Granger."

"That's always dangerous," I said. I was pretty close to him by now.

Cockran's face remained unmoved, regaining its calm. My surprise attacked had startled him, but not for long. "You're hurt."

I lifted the appendage in question. "Cut it on a piece of glass. Afraid I got some blood on the carpet."

Cockran shrugged. "It's Senator Stratterford's carpet. He can afford to have it cleaned or replace it.

Only Cockran separated me from the gun. He began to take a wary step to widen the distance between us. I swung left-handed for his chin, missed, and found myself entangled in his arms. I arched my back and went to my knees and we both tumbled forward. The tile floor ended and we were into the pool. Startled, we let go as we each danced for firm footing on what fortunately turned out to be the shallow end, and then went for each other's throats, madder than wet cats. I tried to not to think about the red tint spreading in the water.

Cockran really wasn't in very good shape. A three pack a day habit and the water didn't help any. I threw another left aimed at his face then grabbed a hank of hair and rammed his head into the concrete edge. The fight was over almost before it began. Breathing hard, I pushed him up into the chrome ladder so that he wouldn't drown, climbed out of the water and stood shakily, applying pressure again to my wrist. I don't know why I was concerned about Cockran living or dying just then considering it all.

"That's quite enough, Granger," Stratterford's voice said behind me.

I drew in a long breath that hurt my chest and turned slowly. My body weighed five hundred pounds and my muscles had turned to rubber. The natatorium's floor tilted beneath my feet. I staggered, caught myself and dropped my chin to my chest. Breathing was a chore. A pool of red colored water grew at my feet, the roar of an ocean building in my ears. I finally raised my head. The gun in Stratterford's hands, I noted wryly, was my very own Smith & Wesson, taken from me earlier by Alexander. It made a little jerk that meant he wanted me to move.

"In front of that window."

I managed to pull myself up straight and walk after a fashion into the cold wind blowing through the broken glass. "I'm supposed to freeze to death?"

I said. "That will be an easy way to explain a body on the property."

"I might let you bleed to death instead. You seem well on your way. Where are the rest of my men?"

"Downstairs, but better not go looking for them unless you have a strong stomach."

He frowned. "That bad?"

"You might say Louis gave his last drop for you, sir. I doubt it was worth the sacrifice."

"And your companions?"

I looked up sharply. So, they had gotten away! I hid my surprise and said, "I don't know. Hopefully as far away from here as they can get in this weather." The frigid air helped settle my head a little, clearing my thinking.

Stratterford gave a small frown. "You stayed behind as a decoy? How very noble of you, Mr. Granger. Or was it stupidity?"

I saw no reason to correct him.

He continued, "No matter. I have more men and it's a very long and cold trek down to town. Few people live this far up the road. They will be apprehended before any further harm is done and your nobleness, Mr. Granger, will have been for no real cause."

I kept pressure on my wrist, the flow had stemmed somewhat, but I'd lost a lot and my head was feeling light, the hammering ache in my head worse now than earlier. I said, "I hadn't planned for it to end quite like this." Over the howl of wind came the raspy whine of the over-revving VW engine. "And frankly, I have no intention letting any *nobleness* go to waste."

Lines etched themselves worriedly in his sun-darkened face. "I have the gun, Mr. Granger, which puts you in a weak position to make predictions."

I forced my voice to speak calmly, casually. I pictured him a student sitting in the front row, all eager to learn something useful, or maybe just hoping to get a good enough grade to put Biology 101 behind him. "The barrel on that gun is four inches long. It's loaded with standard velocity twenty-two long rifle solid point cartridges because that's all I had on hand when I loaded it this morning. You have there the junior member of a very undernourished family of cartridges. The only thing smaller is the twenty-two short—well, there is a wee thing known as a CB Cap, but no one uses it much these days except for punching holes in paper targets in the basement."

It was all blather as I desperately tried to figure a way out of this situation.

"Therefore," I continued, "if you intend to stop me with that peashooter, I suggest you aim either between my eyes or at my heart. Any deviation from those two places will be fatal to you." I was laying it on thick, but what did I have to lose?

"You're shoveling bullshit, Granger." Stratterford wore a cocky smirk. "But I'm not buying it. The news is full of people killed by Saturday Night Specials just like this one. You're not immune."

I laughed, my teeth chattering in the cold air. "You're one dumb Democrat if you think a Smith & Wesson fits in that category, Senator. How did you ever get elected? Sure, a twenty-two will kill you just fine if you're half trying. The problem is, it won't kill fast enough to stop me from snapping enough vertebrae to short circuit every nerve signal to your body. And one more thing...

The distant bark of a .45 caliber pistol cut off my words. I recognize the sound although I'm not sure Mr. Saturday Night Special had any notion what the caliber might be. Three quick bursts, and then a few moments of silence. Our eyes locked. I could see he was thinking. Had the gunshots come from his people? I was pretty sure they hadn't.

And then someone tromped a gas pedal.

"What is that?" I asked.

"The speeder," he replied worriedly.

The raspy note of a four-cylinder air-cooled engine got louder. Stratterford's eyes narrowed and his fingers tightened about the revolver's grips. The speeder must have turned a corner for now the sound of its engine was louder and growing more so by the second. Stratterford had a wild look about him, his eyes darting. "We've talked enough," he said and squeezed the trigger.

The revolver was of the double action variety with a long trigger pull. There was a more accurate method of firing such a gun if one wasn't used to the pull and still keeping the sights on target, but apparently he wasn't familiar with single action shooting, or maybe it was the sound of the approaching speeder that had rattled him enough that he simply forgot.

The .22 made a sharp crack. The next instant a bright red and yellow bathtub burst through the glass wall, its unmuffled engine roaring. Sherri and Brian were hanging onto their seats with terror written all over their faces as the odd-looking device careened across the tile floor, propeller churning up a tornado of flying glass. The speeder slid to a stop on the edge of the swimming pool. Behind the controls Marcie Rose stood and swung the government automatic over the top of the Plexiglas windscreen in a firm, two-handed grip...

Tottering on the edge of the pool, the speeder picked that moment to slip sideways into the water. The propeller whipped a spray to the ceiling, and then the water drowned the engine.

Stratterford fired at Marcie. He missed. Brian gave a sharp cry and fell overboard. I dove for the senator and took him to the floor. There was nothing soft about the Senator from Colorado. I was at least twenty years younger than him, but I fought under a mighty handicap having lost a considerable amount of blood and having just spent five freezing minutes dripping wet in front of a broken window with winter whistling in and around me.

The room began spinning, my vision blurring as I fought to wrestle the gun from his hand. I struck a blow to his chin, and he got one in on me. I felt the impact, but it didn't seem to have an effect. My body had become numb, my nerves reset to a slower speed, my brain flashing a collage of shapes and colors; a warning of impending shut down. Even so, my thinking sharpened as though attempting to compensate, shoving distractions aside to make room for the sole objective, and that was to dispatch Stratterford as speedily as possible before I lost consciousness.

Somehow, I managed to twist the gun from his grip. Heeding my earlier advice, pushed the barrel between the Senator's eyes.

CHAPTER 20

"Stop Granger. Don't do it!"

It wasn't one of those cliché little voices in your head you read about. It sounded damn real and damn urgent, and like a damn fool I paused long enough to listen to it. That's when a hand reached out of the blackness of and grabbed the revolver and shoved it aside. It fired and somewhere, I suppose, the bullet ruined another one of Stratterford's tall windows. And I didn't care. I didn't have the strength or even the will to fight anymore. So in the end, Stratterford's men had swooped in and the Senator had won and I...we'd lost.

Someone was behind me holding my arms, another moving in front of me. I was vaguely aware of his wide, angular face and my revolver in his hand. No longer struggling, what was the use-?, my vision cleared a little; enough to see Marcie scrambling over the edge of the cockeyed speeder, half in and half out of the pool, coloring the blue water in an ugly, black oil slick. Sherri, I noted as if seeing a dream, was doing a labored sidestroke with Brian Landerfelt in a pretty professional looking cross-chest carry. A man in a dark trench coat holding a sawed-off shotgun waited for her at the chrome ladder.

But that was all I could manage. My eyes gave up the fight, the scene became a soft blur and my hearing went haywire.

A man's voice said something; meaningless sounds merging with the ether of unconsciousness....

Consciousness returned briefly some moments later. I was shivering violently beneath a thin blanket, laying on the hard, tile floor, Marcie's blue eyes peering worriedly down at me. Nearby another humped blanket covered another prone body. Sherri was kneeling over it, tangled hair hanging like a wet mop about her shoulders.

"It's going to be all right, Paul," Marcie said soothingly but not very convincingly. I was aware of men standing about, some pretty heavily armed. I tried to speak but only managed to exercise my jaws.

"Don't try to talk."

I had to. She had to know what Stratterford had done with the detonators. I tried again. The room shimmered and faded like a desert mirage.

"He's in shock," someone said.

"We need to move him someplace warm," she snapped. "Where the hell is that ambulance?"

"It's on its way, Marcie. We've stopped the bleeding. Now we wait."

Marcie's voice sounded a bit calmer. "I know, Frank. At least let's move him out of this damn icebox."

"We shouldn't move him at all. You know that. You're not..." I drifted off again as if riding a nitrous oxide-like cloud.

I returned once more during the bouncy ride down the mountainside. A dim light showed we were not all together. Marcie and Sherri were missing. Brian lay on a gurney with two men dressed in white working over him. Apparently, his situation was worse than mine, or maybe I'd been triaged and given a black check mark? I wanted to stay and watch but my body would have none of this foolishness. My brain headed for the exit again, closed the doors, and turned off the light.

CHAPTER 21

"How are you feeling, Paul?" Marcie asked when I finally opened my eyes and saw her sitting on a comfy chair near my bed.

"Awful," I said, "as if that fact isn't self-evident." Sunlight brightening the curtains suggested morning or maybe late afternoon. I had no way of knowing the time, or where I was.

She grinned. "You had that coming, you know."

"Never forget, do you?"

"Like an elephant."

"In more ways than one."

"We can keep my politics out of this," she said jubilantly. Something had gone right for her.

"What are you all cheerful about?"

A smile filled her face. "We did it, you and me. We cracked it open. Stratterford is squawking like a scared parrot, giving us more names than we know what to do with."

That reminded me. "Listen, he told me what he was up to—him and certain persons at STE. The detonators, they've been booby-trapped. They're going to stop working halfway between here and the Soviet Union, or wherever they're aimed. You've got let the military know."

She gave me a patient smile and patted my hand. "Old news, dear. We've known about the sabotage for months."

"You did?"

"Really, Paul, we're much more proficient than you give us credit."

Now I was confused, not that I hadn't been so since that cold morning when she'd come upon my peaceful fishing camp with that old rifle and belligerent attitude. "What about Carl?"

"Poor Carl. Not one of us. He found it out all on his own. He'd pilfered a couple of the components for a stereo receiver he'd designed and was building in his basement. When one of them suddenly stopped working, and a second one did so too. Knowing the implications, he panicked and told me and Alexander, but it was too late by then for me to arrange protection. They ran him down and then took after me because Alexander knew Carl had told me about the faulty components.

I was having trouble putting it together, and still feeling the lingering effects of my concussion didn't help either. "You knew about the switch and allowed it to continue?"

Marcie stood from the chair and gave my shoulder a conciliatory pat. "Easy, Paul, don't get so worked up. You'll pop a vein. You do realize a very dedicated doctor spent his night shift filling you up with fresh blood and stitching you back together."

I remembered the hand. A white gauze bandage encircled it up to my wrist. An IV hose taped to my arm drooped from a bottle of clear fluid dangling on a shiny stand at my bedside. I looked around the room, amazed that I hadn't realized until now that I was in a hospital. A television balanced upon a gooseneck stand sprouting from one wall. A door opened onto a john with a chrome handrail around its dark walls. Farther to the right was another door and a bright hallway beyond. A nurse pushing a cart passed by. Across the hall was another door and someone sitting up in bed watching television.

"We had to maintain the illusion that we didn't know anything," she said sitting gently on the edge of the bed. "We knew Alexander was the inside man, and that Allister had no idea what was happening right under his nose, but we didn't know who was the top dog pulling the strings. Alexander was our only good lead so we made him believe the sabotage hadn't been discovered. All the faulty detonators were kept in a safe place until we could crack this case...and we did. You're not a half-bad partner, partner."

Partner? I didn't much care for the implication in that. I said, "Gee, thanks. Just what I always wanted to do, get back into the espionage game, you really are a spy, aren't you, Marcie Rose. And a pretty deadly rose you are.

"Moi?" She gave me a coy, *little ol' me-?* look.

"Cut the BS. This is me, Paul, remember? The guy you conned halfway across Colorado. I see can right through you now. You're a windowpane, got that. W-I-N-D-O-..."

A man's voice interrupted the spelling lesson.

"You are correct of course, Mr. Granger. Miss Rose is, as you put it, a spy, although we prefer to use a less melodramatic term since Mr. Bond and Helm have glamorized our profession. I call our people 'team members, and never get too specific as to what they do." He stopped by my bed; a tall man with dark, brown hair thinning in front, a sharp-featured face, and thin lips. They were smiling at the moment. Beneath his long, black trench coat he wore a plain brown suit and a gray tie. His hands held a pair of gloves between them.

Marcie said, "Paul, this is Frank Lorring."

Lorring said, "I'm pleased to see you looking well. A big improvement over last night. The doctor indicated you'd lost a considerable amount of blood and scolded me for waiting so long to call an ambulance."

"Your explanation to the doctor was?" I asked.

"You mean about how you managed to cut yourself on the broken skylight over the swimming pool you were attempting to repair? It was adequate to calm his suspicions. The other gentleman's injury was more difficult to explain."

"I suspect it was," I replied evenly.

He went on, "You left us quite a mess to clean up and that will take a bit of creative explaining considering it happened in a prominent Senator's home. Our team members are dealing with the problem now. We'll keep your name out of it...for the moment."

"I appreciate that too. A story like that getting our could cause a stir with the University's president and the board, not to mention the distraction in my classroom next semester."

He studied me a moment and said, "You intend to return to teaching when your sabbatical is over." It was a statement hiding a question.

"Of course," I said seeing that there was something on his mind.

"I've run a check on you. Excellent war record. Eighteen successful missions. Right training and experience, and an uncanny ability to survive. We can make a place in our organization for a man like yourself."

"Who's we?"

He shook his head, a thin smile on his angular face. "If you're interested in joining the team, I'll go into it in more detail. If not, then it's best to let the subject die."

There was a time once, in my younger days, when I would have given the offer serious consideration. Today, I couldn't seem to dredge up that old feeling of excitement, the exhilaration of the hunt like that brief moment on the staircase in an adrenaline spawn longing for 1967 again, another time, another place. That life was over. It had been buried for too long to dig up its corpse and try to breathe life back into it. There were other things that mattered today. I thought of peaceful mountain streams armed only with a good rod and reel, and a box of flies. I thought of teaching, of the smell of a college biology lab... and, curiously, I thought of Sherri too.

I said, "Let it die."

He nodded. "I suspected that might be your answer."

"Will you answer me one question?"

He thought a moment. "That depends on the question."

"How did you happen to show up at Stratterford's place at just the right moment?"

Frank glanced at Marcie. "She called us, told us Stratterford might be the key we've been looking for. We learned his current location, put eyes on the ground, and waited. When you arrived on the plane our people got in touch and we poured every team member available into the area. Of course, that took a little time to organize; several hours. Sorry for the delay."

I looked back at Marcie, freshly scrubbed and combed. She wore a simple blue skirt and matching blue coat over a white blouse. She looked very prim, proper, very first-day-in-class schoolgirlish. She must have gone shopping this morning. I noted the touch of pale pink lipstick and some liner under her eyes. Her cheeks were faintly pink—not from last night's cold air but from a recent encounter with some blush. Looking at her, it was difficult to recall the scraggly, half-frozen woman who only a few days ago stumbled into my fishing camp with a rifle and an attitude. That memory was rapidly fading.

I said, "That was the telephone call you made from the restaurant."

"You see why I couldn't tell you? I didn't want to lie to you, Granger, but I had to. What you didn't know, you couldn't tell to anyone.

A rift had come between us. No more Paul, no more darling. I was Granger again. A very professional, very deadly wall separated us and Marcie was retreating behind it. The gulf had begun to open the moment I'd refused Frank's offer. Marcie had her life, her world, and it was plain my life, my world wasn't going to interfere with it. That was best for both of us, I knew, but at the moment I wasn't sure how I felt about it. At the very least it would be safer like this—for both of us.

"Apology noted and accepted," I said trying to sound light and happy.

A smile fleetingly crossed her lips. "It wasn't an apology, Granger. I just wanted you to know."

"I'd have done the same."

"I know. I was lucky it was you I found on that cold mountain and not some other type of man."

Another type of man? I wondered about that. We both looked over at the sound of footsteps. Sherri stopped just inside the door and stared at Frank and Marcie, suddenly wary. They had apparently impressed upon her their importance—at least their opinion of their importance. I knew the routine; employ a low, even voice and stare with hard, unblinking eyes. Intimidate them with terse, military phrases like *scenario* and *deploy* and *measured retaliation*. Wow the natives with BS and they'll do your bidding like a trained dog. Well, it seemed they had used the tactic on Sherri and she was properly terrified, or was she merely appalled with it all. I felt sorry for her, and I understood a little of her distrust for a system that sired the likes of Frank and Marcie...and me.

She didn't look at me, her view fixed upon Frank like a serving girl waiting to be summoned into the presence of the king. Frank gave his permission in the form of a pleasant smile. Well, why shouldn't he smile? Sherri looked lovely standing there all freshly attired and coifed. "Do come in, Miss Lane," he said beckoned her to enter, showing her his magnanimous side. The gods can be gracious as well as demanding. Sherri was properly awed. Frank might have tried the routine on me too, if he thought for one second it would have worked.

She ventured into the room a little uncertain, and said quickly, "I came to see Paul, but I can come back later if..."

I said, "Come in and join the party. We were just passing the time of day, and by the way, what time is it?"

Sherri was staring at me with that same taunt, wariness she'd given Frank and Marcie, and that bothered me. I was one of them now, no longer the safe, sometimes funny schoolteacher with a penchant for luring innocent fish to their doom. I'd killed a man; cut his throat as emotionlessly as gutting a trout. I was not the same Paul Granger to her—maybe I wasn't the same Paul Granger to myself either, but I'd learn to live with it. Sherri glanced at the Lady Rolex that *daddy* presented to her on her twenty-first birthday. "It's four thirty, Paul, err, a few minutes after."

"Thanks," I said. What I wanted to say was that I hadn't changed, not really...but that would have been a lie.

Frank sensed the tension. He drew in a short breath and said, "I need to be going. Miss Lane, it was nice to have met you. Take care of Paul. He's a good man."

She smiled with effort and took his outstretched hand.

Marcie said, "I've got to get going too. Reports to write, loose ends to tie up. I'll see you later." I knew she wouldn't. When she walked out the door of my hospital room, she walked out of my life forever. We'd come together by chance and now it was time to part. Marcie knew as well as I that outside relationships were dangerous luxuries for a woman in her position. Where she lived was a lonely place. I recalled that aspect of international intrigue vividly, with no regrets for having left it. When you're safe and warm and socially accepted you tend to forget the loneliness of never being able to fully trust another person; the terrible emptiness of never bringing another person into your life for fear of jeopardizing their life.

I looked at Sherri, her small hands clutching a white, knitted handbag, concerned eyes peering down at me, and I knew why I'd turned down Frank's offer. And I was happy.

"How's Brian?" I asked.

"They removed the bullet last night. Doctor Phelps says he'll be good as new." She paused as if not knowing how to continue. "Your doctor says you'll be fine too. I'm glad."

I grinned my usual disarming grin to put her at ease—maybe I was trying to put myself at ease also. "I'm glad too. Turn around."

"What?"

I made the motion with my finger. She complied uncertainly and said, "Well?"

"You've been shopping."

"Everything I had was just ruined. I looked gruesome. Thank goodness we were able to recover my purse and my American Express Card. Breckenridge has some very nice shops."

I smiled. "Just wanted to make sure you hadn't in

desperation bought a pair of jeans that didn't have a designer name and fancy stitching across the back pocket."

"I buy them because they fit me well," she protested.

"Of course. And they do—fit you well, that is."

"You're teasing again." she fitted a playful pout to her carefully *Morning Frosted* lips. It was a better shade of color, I decided, than *Deadly Rose*.

She was the same Sherri Lane and for some reason now that pleased me. I discovered I was a bit startled at the implications. It was nice to know that some things just never change.

A LOOK AT:
THE BEST OF DOUGLAS HIRT

SPUR AWARD WINNING AUTHOR, DOUGLAS HIRT, TAKES YOU THROUGH AMERICA'S WILD WEST IN THIS CAN'T PUT IT DOWN BOXSET.

Captain Ethan Brandish has finally given up his command of Fort Lowell, deep in the Apache territory of Arizona. He knows there has to be more to life than constantly battling rattlesnakes and renegades, and now he's going to find out what life has to offer. But the vicious Apache leader Yellow Shirt has another fate in store for Brandish…

Follow along in these intoxicating stories of love, outlaws, passion, crime and above all else, justice…

The Best of Douglas Hirt includes: *Brandish, Ketcham's Land, The Ordeal of Andy Dean, Devil's Wind, Able Gate and A good Town.*

AVAILABLE NOW

ABOUT THE AUTHOR

Douglas Hirt was born in Illinois, but heeding Horace Greeley's admonition to "Go west, young man," he headed to New Mexico at eighteen. Doug earned a Bachelor's degree from the College of Santa Fe and a Masters of Science degree from Eastern New Mexico University. During this time, he spent several summers living in a tent in the desert near Carlsbad, New Mexico, conducting biological baseline surveys for the Department of Energy.

Doug drew heavily from this "desert life" when writing his first novel, Devil's Wind. In 1991 Doug's novel, A Passage of Seasons, won the Colorado Authors' League Top Hand Award. His 1998 book, Brandish, and 1999 Deadwood, were finalists for the SPUR award given by the Western Writers of America.

A short story writer, and the author of twenty-nine novels and one book of nonfiction, Doug now makes his home in Colorado Springs with his wife Kathy and their two children, Rebecca and Derick. When not writing or traveling to research his novels, Doug enjoys collecting and restoring old English sports cars.